EARTH FRIENDS

PET PROTECTION

HOLLY WEBB

nosy crow

First published in the UK in 2014 by Nosy Crow Ltd
This edition published in 2021
The Crow's Nest, 14 Baden Place
Crosby Row, London, SE1 1YW
www.nosycrow.com

ISBN: 978 1 83994 023 1

Nosy Crow and associated logos are trademarks
and/or registered trademarks of Nosy Crow Ltd

A CIP catalogue record for this book is available from the British Library.

Printed and bound in the UK by Clays Ltd, Elcograf S.p.A.
Typeset by Tiger Media

Papers used by Nosy Crow are made from wood grown in
sustainable forests.

1 3 5 7 9 10 8 6 4 2

MIX
Paper from
responsible sources
FSC® C018072

www.nosycrow.com

ONE

"Shove up a bit." Emily squished herself on to the bench between Maya and the arm. "Oooh, it's cold. I thought this was supposed to be the summer term? I wish I'd brought my gloves."

Poppy nodded. "I know. I took Billy for a walk down by the canal yesterday after school and I nearly froze."

"Is it looking OK?" Izzy asked anxiously. "I haven't been down there for weeks."

"There was a tiny bit of litter – it's OK, Iz, I picked it up! – but no one had dumped anything. And the mural under the bridge still looks great, Poppy."

The four girls had organised a clean-up weekend down by the canal, after Poppy and Izzy had taken Billy down there and he'd got caught up in an old bicycle that someone had thrown into the water. They'd even been on the radio, appealing for people

1

to come and help.

"How could you be cold when you were out with Billy?" Maya asked, nudging Poppy. "He goes so fast, you must have been running to catch up with him."

"I know!" Poppy shivered. "So just think how cold I would have been on my own."

Emily suddenly let out a massive sigh, and the others wriggled round to look at her in surprise.

"What's the matter?" Maya asked, and Emily shrugged.

"Sorry. It was just hearing Poppy talk about Billy. You're so lucky having him. He's gorgeous."

Poppy sniffed. "Some of the time he is."

Izzy giggled. "What did he do?"

"Only ruined one of my sketchbooks," Poppy said grumpily. "I still love him, but it was a close thing for five minutes there."

"How? What happened?" Maya asked, trying not to grin. Billy was a very accident-prone bull terrier, and he always seemed to mix Poppy up in his mess too.

Poppy rolled her eyes. "I was sitting at the kitchen table, just doodling a bit, and I had a couple of biscuits..."

"I get the feeling I know where this is going." Izzy

wrinkled her nose.

"Exactly." Poppy sighed. "Well, I wasn't thinking – it was the drawing, it was really nice, and I sort of forgot, and I left the biscuits at the edge of the table. Billy sniffed them out – he's got a nose like a bloodhound, for food anyway. We could use him to track biscuit thieves, no problem."

"So he ate your biscuits," Emily said, frowning. "I don't see what that's got to do with the sketchbook. Unless he thought that was a biscuit too." Billy was well known for being a bit stupid. Poppy's brothers called him the dumb blond.

"He *didn't* eat the biscuits." Poppy shook her head. "He tried to. But he missed when he jumped up, and he thumped his head on the underneath of the table."

"Oh no! Was he all right?" Emily gasped.

Poppy smiled at her reassuringly. "He was fine. He's got a skull made of wood, Dad says. He was just a bit confused about where his biscuits had gone. But he shook the table up – almost tipped it over. You know how strong he is. And the vase of flowers fell over, and spilled water all across my sketchbook. And me."

"I wouldn't mind. I'd still love a dog like Billy," Emily

said, staring into the distance. She was dreaming about her ideal dog, the others could tell. "Or a cat. A big soft furry one, with a tail like a scarf… Or even a hamster. Well – maybe I wouldn't like a hamster so much, you can't really cuddle a hamster. But any sort of pet would be nice…"

"Jake and Alex have got a friend who wants to sell his pet tarantula," Poppy said brightly.

Emily glared at her. "Any sort of pet *with fur*," she added.

"Oh, Sam says it's *very* furry. And affectionate," Poppy promised her. "It likes to sit on your shoulder."

Emily shuddered. "You know what I mean!"

"Your mum and dad won't let you have a pet at all?" Maya asked sympathetically. She had a huge black cat called Henry, who liked to curl up next to her when she was doing her homework. He was Maya's mum's cat really, but she was off touring or filming so much of the time that he had adopted Maya instead.

"No." Emily shook her head. "I think Dad would quite like to have a dog, but Mum says she would be the one who ended up having to look after it, while he was at work, and we were all at school. She reckons she's got quite enough people to look after, with me and Toby and James and Sukie. And when I tried to explain about it being different, and wanting something to curl up with, she said I was welcome to curl up with Sukie, especially when Sukie woke up at two o'clock in the morning." She slumped down a little on the bench, sighing disgustedly. "And she says if I want to take something for a walk, that's not a problem either, I can just put Sukie in the pushchair."

"Isn't it nice having a little sister?" Maya asked, frowning a little. She was an only child, and quite fancied having someone else around to play with. "You could dress her up. It would be fun…"

Emily stared at her. "You have no idea! Sukie won't wear anything except her wellies. And I mean *just* her wellies. It's a complete battle getting her to wear anything else. She'd rather live in a nappy, her wellies and maybe a woolly hat if she feels a bit cold. I'd love to see you trying to dress her up." Emily snorted with laughter. "She'd probably bite you."

"Oh…" Maya sounded rather downcast. It wasn't what she'd imagined at all.

"I can sort of see your mum's point, though," Izzy said quietly. "There's an awful lot of you in your house already. Have you got room for a dog?"

"A small one…" Emily held out her hands, just a

5

little way apart. "A nice little dog…"

Poppy nodded. "You'd just have to make sure it was really well trained. Not like Billy," she added, before any of the others could say it for her. "Dad took him to lots of training classes, but he never really got the hang of it. You'd need a dog that was very small, and very sensible." She frowned. "I don't know what breed that would be."

Emily shook her head. "Me neither."

"Maybe your mum will let you have a dog when Sukie gets a bit bigger," Maya said, trying to be comforting, but Emily smiled at her lopsidedly.

"I know what she'll say then – that we're all a bit bigger, and there's even less room. I'll just have to keep visiting Billy."

"He can come and have a holiday with you if you like," Poppy volunteered, a bit too eagerly.

Emily giggled. "I don't think that would help convince Mum, would it?"

"Maybe not," Poppy agreed. "Unless you managed to find a really nice small well-behaved dog, and sort of compared it to Billy to make it look even more perfect."

"Yeah, that might work." Emily sighed. "Except I'll never get the chance to try it out."

PET PROTECTION

They were all silent for a moment, thinking.

"Isn't there another way you could have a pet, without actually owning one?" Maya suggested slowly.

"Adopting a zoo animal, you mean?" Emily nodded. "I already have. I've got a snow leopard," she said, rather sadly. "Gran gave me him for my birthday. It's nice – I got a letter about him, and I've got a toy version of him on my bed. But it isn't the same. I've only ever seen him once, and then he was up at the top of his – well, it wasn't a cage. Sort of a big pen with trees and rocks. He wouldn't come down."

"I didn't quite mean that," Maya said. "It was what Poppy said about having Billy for a holiday. Couldn't you be a petsitter? I don't mean having the pets living at your house, but popping in to feed them and give them a cuddle while their owners are away. Or maybe you could take dogs for walks when their owners can't manage it?"

Emily stared at her. "Do you think people would let me?" she asked excitedly. "I mean, I love dogs, and I've got loads of dog books, but I've never actually owned one."

"I bet they would if they saw you with a dog,"

7

Poppy agreed. "You're brilliant with Billy. Anybody could see that you're a dog person." She smirked. "And other pets too, of course. Maybe Sam would like you to pop in and cuddle his tarantula while he goes on holiday." Then she dodged as Emily pretended to smack her.

"Seriously, I bet you could do that. You'd just need to find a way to let people know about you." Maya frowned. "And I suppose you'd really only be able to help out people in Appleby, wouldn't you? Unless your mum would let you go to any of the other villages on your bike."

"I don't think she would." Emily frowned. "She gets panicky about us being out on the roads on our bikes. Which is totally fair when you think about Toby and James, but not for me. But there are lots of people with dogs and cats round our village. Somebody must need a dog-walker."

"You know what else there is in Appleby?" Izzy put in, her pale-blue eyes round with excitement.

The others shook their heads, and Izzy beamed. "The shelter. You know," she added as they looked at her blankly. "The animal shelter! Ummm, it's called Appleby Animal Rescue, or something like that?"

"Oh! Yes, I forgot. But Mum isn't going to let

us adopt a pet from there, Izzy, even though I'd love to," Emily objected.

"I know, I don't mean that," said her friend. "Couldn't you go and help out?"

Emily looked at her blankly for a moment, then she squeaked with excitement. "Why didn't I ever think of that before? I know I'm always saying it, but you're a genius, Izzy!" She jumped up off the bench and hugged Izzy so hard that she squeaked too, and her nose went bright pink, the way it always did when she was pleased.

Emily perched herself on the arm of the bench, frowning thoughtfully. "Today's Thursday, and Toby's got judo after school, so I can't go tonight—"

"Your mum lets him do judo?" Poppy asked disbelievingly. "Like, so he's being *trained* how to fight people? Is that a good idea?"

Emily shrugged. "Apparently, it's supposed to help you calm down – by kicking things, I guess. Who knows. Anyway, we'll have to take him to the sports centre, so Mum'll be trying to cook dinner and everything in a rush. She won't be up for me disappearing off to the animal shelter. But I could definitely go tomorrow afternoon." She bounced excitedly. "Oh, I really hope they do need some help. Even if it's just cleaning out guinea pig hutches or something."

"Will your mum let you do it?" Maya asked suddenly. "I mean, if she's not keen on dogs…"

Emily shook her head. "Oh no, that's the stupid thing. Mum loves dogs. She had a gorgeous Labrador when she was my age. But she says she hasn't got time to look after one properly now. I'm sure she'd be OK with me going to the shelter. Especially if it stops me moaning about having a dog of our own. Oh, I can't wait to go!"

TWO

"Emily, it's me! Maya. I couldn't wait until tomorrow. What did your mum say about helping out at the shelter?"

Maya knew right away how excited Emily was – her words were falling over each other, she was talking so quickly!

"She was fine – she said it was a great idea, and she knows how much I love dogs. Dad said it sounded brilliant, but I had to make sure I still had time for my homework if I go and help at the shelter, because I've already got dancing, but I told them it would be OK. Dancing's only on Mondays, I could help any other night for a bit, or maybe at the weekend."

"So you're definitely going to go and ask tomorrow?" Maya asked.

"Yee-ees," Emily agreed. "That's the only problem. What do I say to them? And what if they say no, they don't want anybody?"

"Mmmm. I should think they'd need as much help as they can get," Maya said thoughtfully. "They'd be more likely to hug you and hand you a bag of dog food. You're not really nervous, are you?"

"A bit," Emily admitted. "It's just the thought of walking in and talking to someone I've never met before…"

Maya *hmmmed* for a moment. "Want me to come with you?" she suggested.

"Yes!" Emily yelped. "I mean, yes, please. Are you sure?"

"I'd like to. I've never been to an animal shelter," said Maya.

"Actually, me neither," Emily admitted. "I'm not sure what it's going to be like."

"Would your mum let you come back to my house tomorrow? You're on the bus on Fridays, aren't you? Then we could go to the shelter together. It's really close to mine."

"Hang on, I'll check."

Maya could hear discussion going on in the background, and what sounded like a full-on fight between Toby and James at the same time. She could see why Emily had said it would be too tricky to get to the shelter tonight. She should have rung later on, she thought to herself crossly. But she'd been so keen to know what Emily's mum and dad had said.

"Yes!" Emily said breathlessly into the phone.

"Sorry! I shouldn't have rung now, your mum's trying to do tea and everything."

Emily giggled. "No, it's fine. James squirted ketchup all over Toby while I was asking her, that's all. She was dithering a bit because she wanted to take me to the shelter so they could see she was OK with the idea, but now she says she'll write me a note, with her mobile number and everything. Then they can call her."

"OK. I'll check with Dad, but I know it'll be fine. He'll come with us, or maybe Anna will if he has to work."

"Is your mum away, then?" Emily asked. She and Poppy and Izzy couldn't help being a little bit curious about Maya's mum, who was a singer called India Kell. She didn't record as much any more, but she did a lot of TV work, and she was always flying off all over the place. (Which made Maya really cross. She was always trying to get her mum to use trains instead, but her mum said it wasn't really practical to get a train to the US, and a boat would take weeks.

She and Maya had agreed that she'd do carbon-offsetting and pay for trees to be planted instead. Maya's mum said this meant that somewhere there was a small forest that belonged to her, and she was planning to build a log cabin in it.)

"Mmmm, she's gone to some awards thing. She's presenting an award for Best New Act. I hadn't heard of any of the people who were up for it, and Mum said she wasn't sure she had either. But one of them had really nice hair, so she reckons he should win. Anyway, she won't be back until Monday."

"I know you don't like it when she's away, but you are lucky, you know..." Emily sighed. "Your dad's there most of the time, and Anna's the best cook. Do you think she'd make chocolate-chip cookies if we asked her really nicely?" Anna was Maya's family's housekeeper. She made gorgeous food, but she didn't approve of Maya being a vegetarian. She cooked lovely veggie stuff for her, but she knew how hard it was for Maya to resist bacon sandwiches, so she was always cooking them for Maya's dad, and wafting the delicious bacon smell all over the house.

"I bet she would. Especially if you ask her, Em. She likes you. She knows you help look after Toby and James and Sukie, and she says children should

14

help out. She thinks I ought to have a little sister or brother, and then I wouldn't be spoilt rotten."

"But you aren't!" Emily told her in surprise. "That's why none of us could really believe it when you said you were India Kell's daughter. When you read about celeb kids, they've always got tiny sports cars, and pet zebras and things—"

Maya snorted with laughter.

"I'm serious! Or they've got half of Chelsea football team coming to help at their birthday party or something like that. You're normal. Well. Almost normal, anyway," Emily added sweetly. She was on the phone, so Maya couldn't slap her. "You do have your own laptop – which I'd kill for, by the way – and a mobile, and your house is enormous, but otherwise, you're not that different from me and Poppy and Izzy."

"I love you too," Maya said, still trying not to laugh. "Anyway. Tomorrow at mine, and I'll make Dad come with us. He could do with a walk."

✦

"Do you think they'll say yes?" Emily asked anxiously, for about the fifth time since they'd set off.

"Yes!" Maya rolled her eyes.

"I think they'd be really glad of the help, Emily,"

Maya's dad put in. "The shelter's pretty tiny, and I'm sure I remember seeing an article about it in the paper – it's mostly run by one lady, and she's really overworked."

Appleby Animal Rescue was an old farmhouse, just outside Appleby village, where Emily and Maya both lived. It was a nice-looking house, not very big, but with a square yard in front of it, with stables and outhouses all round.

"Do you think all those building have got animals in them?" Emily asked, looking around in surprise. "I didn't think it would be this big."

"I suppose there isn't another animal shelter anywhere close," Maya said thoughtfully. "Any abandoned animals would have to come here." She nudged Emily. "So, are we going in?"

Emily pushed the big wooden gate open. There was a sudden excited chorus of barking, and the two girls looked at each other in surprise.

Maya's dad laughed. "Wow, the dogs know to listen for the gate opening, don't they? Maybe they think we're bringing them treats."

"At least it means someone knows we're here. Look." Maya nodded towards a friendly-looking woman in a pair of very dirty jeans who was hurrying across the yard towards them.

"Hello! Are you wanting to look at the animals? A dog, maybe?" She sounded really hopeful, and Emily wished so much that they were.

"No, um…" She took a deep, gasping breath and gave Maya a panicky look, who nodded enthusiastically. "I was wondering if you needed any help? I live quite close, and I love dogs, and cats too. I could come after school, maybe, or at the weekend?"

"Oh…" The lady looked at her consideringly, and Emily was glad that she'd brought clothes to change into at Maya's house, sensible clothes that looked quite like what the lady from the shelter was wearing, except cleaner. Maya had put a sparkly top on (practically everything she owned was sparkly apart from her school uniform, Emily reckoned), but Emily had suggested she needed a hoodie on over the top, so most of it was hidden. She looked like a reasonably sensible friend for someone who wanted a volunteer job at an animal shelter.

"What's your name?" the lady asked.

"Emily. Emily Harris. And this is Maya."

"I'm Maya's dad, Tom Knight," Maya's dad added, holding out his hand for the lady to shake, but she laughed, and shook her head instead.

"I'm really sorry, I've got horrible dirty gloves on, you don't want to! I'm Lucy, I run the shelter." She smiled at Emily. "So … you want to come and help. Do you have a dog at home?"

Emily shook her head. "No. Does that matter?" she asked sadly. "I'd love a dog, but my mum thinks we're all too busy to look after one. It was Maya and my other friends at school who said maybe I could work at the shelter instead. I like cats too," she added quickly.

"It doesn't matter at all – I just wondered what gave you the idea, that's the only reason I asked. Sometimes people come and help out because they've had a dog or a cat from a shelter, and they realise how much work we do."

"Do you really run this whole place on your own?" Maya's dad asked, looking around in amazement. All the buildings around the farmyard had been converted into small pens and they all looked full.

"I'm the only person who's here all week," Lucy agreed. "But I have a lady who comes in to do the office work every morning, and some volunteers who pop in on different days."

"But if one of the dogs was ill, you might be up

all night – and then you'd have to do everything the next day as well!" Emily said worriedly. She'd seen how tired her mum got when one of them was sick and she didn't get any sleep – it meant she wandered around like a ghost the next day, and Emily had to remind her about things like packed lunches and teeth-brushing.

"Mmm. Luckily it doesn't happen all that often, but it's awful when it does. We've got a beautiful spaniel cross who took the whole night to have six puppies a few weeks ago. I was so tired the next day that I ended up feeding half the dogs cat food." Lucy smiled. "Luckily they didn't seem all that bothered."

Emily sighed blissfully. "There are puppies!"

"Yes…" Lucy sighed. "They're really gorgeous – but six more dogs to find homes for."

Emily nodded wistfully. "I'd love a puppy, but my mum's right – my baby sister's too little. If we had a dog it would have to be a nice, calm older dog who wouldn't mind if Sukie tried to feed it Lego. Sukie's my little sister," she added. "She's two."

"Oh, I see." Lucy nodded. "Well, some dogs are good with little children, but not all of them. Your mum's just being sensible." She looked at Emily and Maya for a moment. "Do you want to come and see some of the animals?"

Emily nodded enthusiastically. Lucy hadn't said yes to wanting a helper, but at least if she was letting them look around, it must mean she wasn't totally against the idea?

She followed Lucy in through one of the doors set around the edge of the yard, and blinked as they came in out of the bright sunlight outside.

"This used to be the dairy," Lucy explained.

The long, low building ran all along one side of the yard. It was a line of pens, opening out on to a passageway, and each pen had a dog or maybe two inside. As they saw Lucy and Emily and the others, they leapt up excitedly, scratching at the wire fronts of the pens, and barking.

"So many!" Maya murmured, as she looked down the long passage.

"We're quite full at the moment," Lucy agreed. "Twenty-three dogs. That's including the six puppies though."

"Do you get lots of visitors wanting to rehome them?" Maya's dad asked, crouching down to let a pretty little Jack Russell lick his fingers through the bars.

Lucy sighed. "Not enough, to be honest. That little

one – Posy, we call her – she'd make a gorgeous pet. But even though we put the details up on the website, we just don't get enough people coming to see us. Four or five visitors a week, usually. We've had Posy for nearly a month now."

"Must be expensive to keep them all – the food, and paying to keep these pens warm." Maya's dad reluctantly said goodbye to Posy, and moved on to look at the elderly Labrador in the next pen. He was sitting down, about the only dog that was, but he was thumping his huge black tail on the concrete floor, and panting excitedly.

"This is Barney. He's a darling – his owner couldn't look after him any longer, because he had to move in with his daughter's family. It's a huge change for an old dog like Barney, coming here, but he's been so good." Lucy stroked him, and Barney closed his eyes and slobbered happily. "He's going to be hard to rehome. Everyone wants puppies, you see. Not a grand old man like Barney."

"You shouldn't have brought me here, Maya," her dad muttered. "I could take the lot of them home. He's great."

"Anna would have a fit," Maya pointed out. "Mum too. And Henry would never speak to us again."

Emily was further down the passage, murmuring lovingly to a little whippet, who was eyeing her shyly from the corner of the pen.

"She's so pretty," she whispered to Lucy. "But so tiny and thin!"

"Oh, be careful…" Lucy hurried down the passage to her. "Twinkle's pretty nervous, and she does sometimes snap…" But she stopped as she came up behind Emily, and saw Twinkle tiptoe towards her, and let Emily rub her beautiful satiny ears.

"Her nose tickles." Emily giggled as Twinkle gently nosed at her hands, and licked her.

"Well…" Lucy said quietly. "Wow. She doesn't even do that for me. She's the shyest little thing. We decided someone must have scared her quite badly."

Emily looked up at Lucy worriedly. "Oh! I hope it was OK to stroke her." She started to pull her hand back through the wire door of the pen, but Twinkle was still sniffing and licking at her.

"Don't stop! She really likes you." Lucy eyed her, frowning. "Look, I'd love for you to come and help out at the weekends, but you do realise we can't pay you, don't you? I'd like to be able to, but we're desperately short of money, and the roof in here's leaking." She nodded towards a bucket in the corner.

22

"It really needs mending before this winter comes. I just couldn't afford to pay you."

"Oh, I don't want to be paid," Emily said in a surprised voice. Then she laughed. "I'd pay *you* if it meant I got to hang around with the dogs. And I meant to say, I brought a letter from my mum, with her phone number and everything, saying it's OK for me to help."

Lucy nodded. "That's a good idea. I'll call her, just to say hello. So she knows who I am." She smiled at Emily, and at Maya who'd come up behind them. "Well, if you're going to help, you'd better come and meet everybody else."

"There's more?" Maya said, surprised.

Lucy laughed. "Oh yes. Another whole big area for cats – that's the old stables. And we've got quite a lot of guinea pigs, a couple of rabbits, and even a pony. Oh, and the chickens."

"Chickens? At an animal shelter?" Emily stared at her in surprise as they started to cross the yard.

"Mmm-hmm. They're rescued battery hens."

"Wow," Emily muttered. "I thought just dogs and cats. I never knew you had all these other animals."

Lucy shrugged. "Well, I never meant to have the chickens. Someone just rang up and said could we take the first lot, and I couldn't say no… They're over there, you see?" She pointed across to a path that ran along the side of the farmhouse to a little garden, with a fenced chicken run. The girls could see a few black and red hens strutting about. Then Emily blinked.

"Um… What sort of chicken's that?"

Lucy glanced round. "I'm not really sure. The battery hens tend to be a mixture."

"But she's stripy! I didn't know hens could look like that." Emily pointed out the rainbow-striped chicken to Maya, and Lucy suddenly laughed.

"Sorry! I'm so used to seeing them like that I forgot you wouldn't know. She's got a jumper on. Battery hens get their feathers pecked out sometimes, or they just lose them from being squashed up in the cages. The jumpers are to keep them warm until their feathers grow again. There's a lady in the village who knits them for us."

Emily giggled. "You see, Maya, you should come and volunteer too. You could give the hens fashion advice."

Maya chuckled, but she was looking thoughtful.

"These are the cat pens." Lucy held the door open for the girls to look in, and Maya gasped.

24

PET PROTECTION

"Oh, he looks just like Henry!"

Emily nodded. The large black and white cat in the pen nearest the door could have been Henry's brother. He was lounging on a shelf attached to the side of the pen, with a fat, rather tatty-looking cushion on it. There were cat toys scattered around the floor, but the Henry lookalike didn't seem very interested in them. He stared at Emily and Maya, and yawned hugely, showing needle-sharp teeth.

"Definitely like Henry," Maya giggled.

"Only nine cats at the moment," Lucy said. "Not too many. Most of them are in this big pen together over here, but Whiskers – the big black and white chap – isn't the most sociable." She sighed. "He beats the others up. So he has his own pen."

"Do they ever get to go out of the pens?" Maya asked. She couldn't imagine Henry staying shut up in a small pen – he'd hate it.

Lucy nodded. "We have an exercise area that backs on to the pens, with a sort of assault course for them to climb on. But they have to take turns. Someone's coming to see Whiskers tomorrow though," she added hopefully. "They saw him on the website. You never know. He's lovely with people, he's only a big bully to other cats. Anyway. Come and see the guinea pigs, they're just next door."

The guinea-pig room was one big mass of hay and fur as the guinea pigs skittered about, squeaking and chirruping as they nosed for the bits of carrot that were hidden in their bedding. They made Emily laugh, they were so round and cute, and most of them were very tame. They let Emily and Maya pick them up, and one fluffy ginger one flaked out and went to sleep on Maya's dad.

Lucy looked at Emily hopefully. "So. You still want to come and help? Would you like to come tomorrow?"

"Yes! Yes, please!" Emily said eagerly. "And I don't mind what I do. I can clean runs, anything."

"I'll probably get you to exercise the dogs," Lucy said thoughtfully. "We just don't have enough time to walk them all properly. We're lucky that we've got lots of space – we can take them out for lovely walks without even going off the shelter site, if we can only find the time."

Emily nodded. "That sounds great. You're lucky having such a beautiful place for the shelter – the animals are lucky to end up here too."

Lucy sighed. "I know. It's a great place. I've worked here for about five years, and I love it. I used to work

26

with Steve, he started the shelter and turned it into a charity. That was almost exactly ten years ago now. This was the farm his family had run for years and years, you see. And when he died he left the house and all the buildings to the charity in his will, with a little bit of money to pay the manager – that's me. The problem is that the buildings are pretty old, and shabby, and we've not got a lot of spare money for fixing them up. I don't know how we're going to get that roof mended, but we really need to." She shook her head anxiously. "Sometimes I worry that we'll have to close."

"But you couldn't!" Emily gasped. "There isn't anywhere else for all the animals to go!"

"I know. We always keep going somehow." Lucy smiled at her. "Something always turns up."

THREE

"Would you mind if I came too?" Maya asked Emily, as they walked back to her house.

Emily had been wandering along in a dream, smiling to herself, and thinking about the animals at the shelter. The spaniel puppies had been particularly gorgeous. They were still really tiny, so they were living with their mum in the farmhouse kitchen, where Lucy could make sure they stayed warm. They were white, with brown patches, and pink, squashed noses, and although they could walk, they weren't very good at it. They kept blundering around and falling over each other.

"Mmmm?" Emily said vaguely. "Oh! That would be great! It would be really nice if we both did it."

"You don't want it to be just your thing?" Maya suggested, a little anxiously.

But Emily laughed. "I think Lucy needs all the

help she can get."

"Would it be OK with you, Dad?" Maya asked hopefully, as they got home and he started to open the front door.

Her dad nodded. "Sounds great. It could be a lot of hard work though, girls."

"We'd only be doing it on a Saturday morning," Emily reminded him. "It's not like being there all week."

"True. You two have got about an hour before I said I'd take Emily back, by the way. I'll ask Anna to get your tea on."

The girls headed upstairs, and curled up on the little sofa in Maya's room.

"I can't wait to go back to the shelter tomorrow," Emily said.

"I know!" But Maya was frowning. "But it's a bit scary what Lucy was saying about the roof, and not having enough money to keep the shelter going, isn't it? I hope something does come along like she said it would. Or all those poor dogs and cats might end up homeless."

"And the chickens." Emily shook her head. "I still can't get over that chicken in a jumper. But if it closes down, who's going to give a home to a bald chicken?" She sank her chin in her hands. "Do you think there's a way we could help raise money for the shelter? Like the fashion show we did to raise money for the Fairtrade clothes people?"

Maya nodded. "I was thinking that. Not a fashion show, of course. Although…" She rummaged in the pile of magazines balanced precariously on the arm of the sofa. "Look! I knew I remembered seeing this! I stuck a pencil in the page because it was so cute – but sort of scary at the same time."

Emily looked at the photo and made a face – it was a dog, probably a Border terrier, she guessed. And it was wearing a coat. She'd seen lots of dogs in coats out walking in the winter – usually sensible navy or black ones, but every so often she spotted a dog in a loud red tartan, or even a flowery print coat. But nothing like this. This dog coat was pink, with a fluffy feather trim all round the edge, and the dog's name (Lulu) spelled out in diamanté sparkles. There was a matching feathery headband as well. The dog did not look happy.

"I bet it isn't really called Lulu," Maya said.

Emily giggled. "In fact, it's probably a boy."

"Anyway. We couldn't do a fashion show again, but there must be something special we could organise.

30

Something that would raise loads of money..." Maya wrinkled her nose. "But I can't think of it."

"Mmmm..." Emily frowned, and flicked through the magazine. But it was full of photos of people at smart parties, and film premieres, and no use for thinking about an animal shelter. "Could we get sponsored to do something?" she asked vaguely.

Maya nodded thoughtfully. "Walking the dogs, maybe? Fifty pence a mile? But I'm not sure that would raise very much money, if it was just the two of us. Roofs are expensive to mend."

"I know. It has to be something big," Emily sighed. "And really fun. I know!" She sat up suddenly, dislodging Henry, who'd been sitting on the arm of the sofa looking grand. He hit the floor with a thump of paws, and shook himself furiously before he stalked out of the room.

"Sorry, Henry!" Emily called after him, and then she turned back to Maya. "What about a party? A birthday party for the shelter? Lucy said it was set up almost exactly ten years ago."

"But how does a party raise money?" Maya asked. "They cost loads! Mum always starts complaining if she has a party. She says they're astronomical."

Emily sniffed. "That's because your mum's parties

mean huge guys in black suits doing security, and hiring a field from the farmer next door so people can land their helicopters. Most of us just buy a few crisps, Maya. Anyway, I meant the kind of party that you sell tickets for. And then you have competitions, games, that sort of thing. Sort of a cross between a party and a school fair."

Maya was nodding excitedly. "Yes! And we could say it was a completely animal-friendly party! Use free-range eggs in the cake, and that sort of thing!"

"Does that mean all vegetarian? No ham sandwiches?" Emily asked suspiciously. She understood why Maya wanted to be a vegetarian, but she was sure she couldn't be one herself. It would be way too hard.

"Only ham sandwiches made out of happy pigs," Maya said firmly. "Ones with nice outdoor sheds, and lots of mud to roll around in."

"Is there really such a thing as happy pigs?" Emily said in a disbelieving voice. "It sounds like you made that up."

"I did not! There's a farm not that far from here that's actually famous for its happy pigs. So we can have happy ham sandwiches."

"OK…" Emily agreed. "So now we just have to

tell Lucy tomorrow that we're organising a party for her."

"Mmmm, I know. And we haven't even started helping out yet. Maybe we ought to wait till we've actually been there for the whole morning, or she's going to think we're really bossy…"

◆

"Did you have a good time? Was Twinkle OK?" Lucy asked the girls anxiously, as they came back into the main yard.

"She was fine," Emily told her. "She did stop and sniff absolutely everything, though. I don't think we actually walked all that far."

"And I'm not sure Barney really likes walking," Maya said. "He walks for about three steps, and then he sits down."

"But luckily that's usually when Twinkle starts to sniff something, so they're pretty good to walk together." Emily crouched down to rub Twinkle's ears. "Did you have a nice time, mmm? Did you smell lots of good smells?"

"Well done." Lucy looked quite relieved. "Do you want to put them back in their pens, and then it's almost time for you to go home."

Emily stared at her disbelievingly. "It can't be!

We've hardly done anything!"

Lucy laughed. "It's nearly twelve, honestly, and you've been here since eight."

Emily and Maya had helped Lucy to feed everyone when they first arrived, and then they'd hosed down a couple of the dogs' pens before they set off to walk Twinkle and Barney. The morning had just disappeared. Walking the dogs had definitely been the best bit, Emily thought. They'd stomped across a very muddy field (her wellies might never be the same again) to the little wood. She and Maya had chatted a bit, but not all the time, and it had been wonderful watching Twinkle skittering about. She was more like a butterfly than a dog, Emily reckoned. She definitely fluttered everywhere. And Barney plodded, but he was still a darling. She'd loved being with the dogs just as much as she'd hoped she would. She couldn't wait for next week.

"Have you got a minute, before we have to go?" Emily asked, glancing at Maya.

Lucy looked worried. "Of course. What's the matter?"

"Nothing! Actually, I was going to ask if you wanted me to come tomorrow as well," Emily added hopefully. "But that wasn't the main thing.

34

We had an idea…"

Maya nodded. "For fundraising, for mending the roof."

"We were thinking maybe the shelter could have a birthday party," Emily suggested shyly. "A tenth birthday *is* quite special. We could make it a big thing, and sell tickets."

Lucy looked at them doubtfully. "I don't know. It is a lovely idea, but I just don't have time to organise that sort of thing. It would take a lot of work."

"We know!" Emily nodded. "We meant we'd do it. Honestly, we could. We organised a fashion show before."

"And we got people to clean up part of the canal in Millford. We're very good at running things," Maya said, trying to sound confident. "We were thinking an animal-friendly party. So all the food would be from cruelty-free farms. And we'd use Fairtrade stuff too."

Lucy nodded. "I like the idea a lot, if you can actually get people to buy the tickets… And we'd have to hire a hall, I suppose? Maybe you could make the food local, as well – you know, saving on food miles."

"Oh yes! Mr Finlay talked about that at school," Emily agreed, "Not buying potatoes flown in from

South America when there's a farm down the road that sells them. Good idea." She beamed at Lucy. "So you think yes then? We can start planning the party? Maybe we could have it in the summer half-term, that's about six weeks away."

Lucy looked faintly worried, but she nodded. "Yes. I suppose that's OK. If you're really sure you can organise all this."

Emily crossed her fingers behind her back. "Oh, we can…"

✦

"You know, I'm sure we *can* sort out everything for a big party, it's getting the people to buy tickets for it that's going to be the problem," Emily said thoughtfully to Maya, as they sat in the school bus on Monday morning.

Emily had gone to the shelter again on Sunday, but Maya's dad had planned a trip to London to cheer her up while her mum was away, so they hadn't had a chance to do any more party planning.

"Mmmm." Maya stared out of the window. "People need to know that it's happening. We need posters. Something really cute, with all the animals on…"

"We need Poppy," Emily agreed. "She'd be able to

draw something brilliant. We could take photos of the real animals at the shelter for her to work from."

"Awww, she could draw the chickens with the jumpers on!" Maya laughed. "Or maybe Honey and her gorgeous puppies. Poppy would help out, wouldn't she? We'd only have to tell her about all those homeless dogs."

"Perhaps we shouldn't – she'd try and persuade the rest of her family to adopt them all," Emily pointed out. "Her mum might never speak to us again. Maya, do you think Izzy might like to help as well? I know she's not as much of an animal person, but she's so brilliant at organising things and doing lists. She'd be fantastic for a party planner."

Maya nodded. "Definitely. You know, I think if me and Izzy went into partnership, we could be the best party planners ever. She could do all the actual organisey planning bits, and I could have the mad ideas."

"What about me?" Emily asked indignantly.

Maya elbowed her. "You could shout at the clients when they change their minds and say they've decided on a Venetian banquet theme instead of the cool New York look they wanted yesterday."

Emily sighed. "I can't help it. I get a lot of practice

shouting at Toby and James. I haven't had a go at any of you for ages."

"Actually, you're right, you haven't. I should think helping out at the shelter will make you feel less like arguing with people anyway," Maya suggested. "Dogs are very … therapeutic. Which means they make you feel better. Like those dogs that go to hospitals just so people can stroke them."

"Wouldn't Barney be good at that?" Emily said, smiling. "He'd just sit there, and thump his tail and let his tongue hang out. He's like a big black teddy bear. So – shall we ask Izzy and Poppy if they'll help? It would be fun to do another big project together anyway. And we can tell Mr Finlay. He told me the other day that he thought we might be ill because we hadn't asked him to arrange anything really tricky for ages."

They hurried off the bus – after Emily had found both her little brothers, and sent them back to fetch all the stuff they'd left behind – and went to look for Izzy and Poppy.

"How was the animal shelter?" Poppy yelled excitedly, as she saw them coming. "Did you go? Did they say yes? Are you going to help out?"

"Yes." Emily grinned at her. "To all the questions.

PET PROTECTION

It was brilliant, and Maya's going to help too. Every Saturday morning, and maybe Sundays sometimes as well."

"There's Izzy!" Maya pointed across the playground, and they saw Izzy coming in the gate. Emily waved wildly at her. It would be easier only to explain about the party once, she thought.

"Did you go to the shelter?" Izzy demanded, as soon as she got close enough.

"Yes, you're a total genius, and it was a brilliant idea." Emily hugged her, and Izzy looked surprised, but pleased. She stood there a bit stiffly, and let herself be hugged. She and Emily hadn't got on all that well when Izzy had first joined their group to work on the class's Fairtrade project, and she sometimes wasn't sure Emily liked her as much as the others did.

"But now," Emily glared at her sternly, "we need you to help. You too, Poppy," she added. "The shelter's amazing, but it's really short of money, and we were thinking we could have a sort of fundraising party. It's the shelter's tenth birthday this year." She looked at them both hopefully. "So … please? Will you help organise it too? We're brilliant when we all do things like this together."

Izzy took off her backpack and reached into one

of the pockets, bringing out a little notebook with a pencil on a string. She folded the cover over and looked at Emily in a businesslike way.

Emily laughed. "I knew you'd help organise us."

"When are you thinking it should be?" Izzy asked.

"Sometime in the summer half-term," Maya explained. "That gives us lots of time to plan everything, *and* to make sure that people know about it. That's where you come in," she told Poppy. "Posters!"

"Really cute, gorgeous fun posters for the best party day out ever!" Emily agreed.

"OK." Poppy nodded.

"You'd be fantastic at designing any decorations too," Maya added.

"Where's it going to be?" Izzy asked, sitting down on one of the benches so that she could scribble in her notebook better. "What sort of decorations will will we be putting up?"

Maya and Emily looked at each other anxiously. "That's the only thing," Emily admitted. "We don't actually know where we're going to have it."

"If it was nice weather we could just use the yard at the shelter," Maya explained. "But if it rains that would be useless. And there isn't really anywhere else

– just lots of pens, and the house, and that doesn't have any big rooms for a party."

Izzy frowned. "Hiring a hall would probably be really expensive."

"Oh, no, we can't do that!" Emily said. "We need to raise money, not spend it…"

"And we don't have any money at all, until we've sold some tickets," Maya sighed. "Anyone who owned a hall would want us to pay them when we book, I should think."

"But then what are we going to do?" Emily asked. They couldn't give up already. She thought of Twinkle, and Barney, and Honey and the puppies. They needed that money!

Izzy shook her head, and then slipped her notebook back into her bag as the bell rang for registration. "We'll just have to find somewhere that doesn't cost anything," she said. "There must be places…"

Emily nodded, but she still felt miserable. She couldn't think of anywhere at all.

FOUR

"I nearly forgot! Look what I've made for you!"
Poppy leaned over their table, and passed Emily a
piece of card, carefully sealed in a plastic envelope.
"I scanned it on Mum's scanner too, so I'll email it
to you when I get home. But I just wanted you to see
the real thing first."

Emily took it, wondering what on earth it could be,
and Maya and Izzy peered over to see too. Mr Finlay
hadn't arrived yet – he was always losing stuff in the
staffroom, and he often turned up out of breath and
trailing piles of paper.

"Oh, Poppy! You made me a logo!" Emily said
delightedly, turning the envelope so that the others
could look at it properly. "That's so clever, *and* it
actually looks like me."

The little picture showed Emily with her trademark
curly bunches, wearing a T-shirt with a heart on it,

and with her arms around a cat and a dog – the dog had curly ears and looked like Honey, the spaniel at the shelter.

Poppy nodded, pleased. "I was thinking last night that you really ought to try out Maya's idea, and be a petsitter. You'd be so good. So I thought you'd need a leaflet, with a cute logo. If you get really successful, you could even have business cards," she added.

"This is brilliant… What else do you think I should put on the leaflet?" Emily asked. "Normally when we get stuff like that through the door they say they've got twenty years' experience at gardening, or whatever it is. And I haven't got any."

Izzy nodded. "Mmmm. My dad's leaflet says that. And, um, *All types of garden work undertaken. No job too small. References available on request.*"

"What does *that* mean?" Emily asked, wide-eyed.

"It means that if you want he can give you my auntie's phone number and she'll tell you he's brilliant." Izzy giggled.

"Oooh, you should definitely say that. You could put Billy as a reference!" Poppy said excitedly. "He'd say you were fab. Well, I mean, I would for him."

"And maybe if you asked Lucy, she'd let you give her name, or the shelter's," Maya suggested. "She was really pleased with you at the weekend, wasn't she?"

Emily nodded. "Yes. She seemed to be, anyway. I might leave it till I've done a couple more weekends before I ask her, though. Poppy, do you think your mum would mind if people rang you up to ask if I was a good petsitter?"

"I shouldn't think so," Poppy said, frowning. "You came over and fed him for us when we went away for the weekend, didn't you? That counts as petsitting. And you've walked him lots with me. I'll ask Mum, maybe she'll agree to say it, if anyone rings. It would probably sound better coming from a grown-up. She can definitely say nice things about you. Anyway, she's known you for what, five years? She can say you're honest and reliable and um, clean, and stuff."

"Clean?" Emily rolled her eyes.

Poppy shrugged. "Well, people might want to know that you won't take their dogs out and then stomp mud all over their carpets."

Emily nodded, looking worried. "I hadn't thought of that. I suppose there's all sorts of things that might go wrong. I mean, what if I take someone's dog to the woods, and he slips his lead? And I never find him again!"

44

PET PROTECTION

"Ems! You haven't even got a dog-walking job yet!" Maya elbowed her. "Stop being such a drama queen. Just concentrate on making a smart leaflet first."

"I suppose I am getting a bit over the top…" Emily murmured. "It's just such a big responsibility." Then she smiled. "But it would be so nice if I actually did get some customers. I could easily walk a couple of dogs after school. Maybe even before school if I got up really early." She glanced over at the door to check Mr Finlay still wasn't coming, and then hopped up and ran round the table to hug Poppy. "You're totally, utterly brilliant. I'm going to go home and design the nicest leaflets. And a business card as well, just in case." She grinned, imagining handing out her card to sweet-looking dogs she met in the street, and then scooted back to her seat as Mr Finlay finally arrived, looking harassed.

✦

"Mum, please! It's my turn, it's been my turn for ages, and Toby and James won't get off the Lego website."

Emily's mum put her head round the door of the tiny room where the computer lived, and sighed. "All right. You two. Off. Emily's right, it's her turn. And you need to go and have a bath, anyway."

"But we're in the middle of a level!" Toby howled

45

furiously. "You can't make us stop now! That's just so mean!"

"Really mean!" James chimed in, agreeing with his big brother for once. "I had a bath yesterday, anyway."

"You didn't." Toby turned round and smirked at him. "You just stuck your head under the tap and told Mum you got in the bath." Then he groaned. "Oh, look, now we died! Mu-uuum! You made us die! We'll have to start again now." He settled back on the chair, darting a smug little glance at Emily. Toby always went with possession being nine-tenths of the law – it would be much easier for Mum just to say, *Oh, you don't mind, do you, Emily?* than it would be to make him move...

"No!" Emily dug her nails into her palms to stop herself yelling at Toby – or grabbing him and pulling him away from the computer, which was what she really felt like doing. If Mum took his side, she was going to scream.

Emily glanced round at Mum anxiously. Sometimes she just didn't notice how Emily was feeling, and that made Emily crosser than anything – knowing that Mum was worrying about whether Sukie had eaten any tea, or if Toby had got into trouble with his teacher again, or what time Dad was getting home from work. Emily knew that Mum did have a lot to worry about, but she got sick of being the one that Mum *didn't* have to fuss over. It would be nice if all Mum's attention was on her for once.

Mum patted her shoulder, and glared at Toby, and Emily took a deep breath of relief.

"Toby, get off the computer now and go and get in the bath! If you argue with me about it again you won't be playing on it tomorrow, either."

Toby stomped away growling, and James looked thoughtfully at the screen, and then at Mum, and decided it would be sensible to follow him.

"Thanks, Mum." Emily smiled at her gratefully.

"Sorry you had to wait, sweetheart. Are you trying to do some homework?"

"Ummm, not quite," Emily murmured. "I think Poppy sent me an email, that's all." It was all very well having Mum's attention, but actually, Emily didn't really want to tell her about the petsitting and dog-walking plan just yet. She glanced around, trying to think of some way to distract her. Then she frowned, and looked up at the ceiling.

"What is it?" her mum asked worriedly. "Can you hear something upstairs? Oh no, Toby and James are probably splashing water all over the bathroom. Sorry, Ems, we'll talk about your homework later."

Emily hadn't actually heard anything, but she didn't feel guilty about getting her brothers into trouble. They almost certainly were splashing water all over the bathroom. They couldn't even *look* at water without splashing it.

Happily, she clicked on the attachment from Poppy, and started trying to make up her leaflet. Poppy had sent her a photo too, one she'd taken of Emily and Billy a couple of months before. She'd called the file *A Satisfied Customer*. Emily grinned. That was a great idea.

Emily had borrowed a couple of leaflets from the board in the kitchen where Mum pinned up the numbers for the plumber and other useful stuff, and she was planning to look on petsitters' websites too, to get some more ideas.

No one had a logo as nice as hers, she decided, a few minutes later. But there were an awful lot of petsitters, and they all seemed to have years and years of experience. Still, at least there didn't seem to be anyone else very close by, although there was one lady in Millford who said she could do calming massage and aromatherapy for cats who were missing their owners. Emily wondered if she knew Poppy. She thought they might get on.

Carefully, she checked all her spelling, and then twirled a strand of her dark, curly hair round her finger. Was she really ready to do this? It sounded such a good idea, but a bit scary too. Then she remembered how much fun it had been walking Twinkle and Barney with Maya at the weekend. She'd loved it, and Twinkle had too. Lucy had said that Twinkle hadn't had a proper walk in ages. What if there was another dog out there like Twinkle, with an owner who couldn't manage to exercise her properly? It would be brilliant to be able to help out dogs like that. She really wanted to.

Maybe she should take out the petsitting bits in her leaflet, and just concentrate on the dog-walking, Emily mused. No matter what the others said, Emily wasn't sure that people would really want to give their door keys to a ten-year-old while they were on holiday. And holidays only happened once or twice a year, too. If she had a couple of regular dogs to walk, that would be much better. Almost like having her own dog. Twinkle was gorgeous – but so gorgeous that surely she would be adopted soon. Lucy had already warned Emily not to get too attached to any of the animals.

Emily smiled to herself, imagining taking a dog on some of her favourite walks – along by the edge of the stream that ran past Maya's house would be great. It would be even better going on her own, without Toby and James fighting and splashing and trying to push each other in, and Mum panicking about Sukie's pushchair getting stuck in the mud.

And a regular walking job would earn her some money, too, Emily realised suddenly. She'd put how much she would charge down on the leaflet, of course, but she hadn't really imagined having the money. She could save up for a dog of her own, perhaps. Surely one day she'd be able to persuade Mum?

Quickly Emily took out the bits she didn't need, and made the photo of her and Billy a bit bigger to fill up some of the space. Then she hit print, and crossed all her fingers together into complicated knots...

✦

Emily had been hoping that as soon as she had delivered her leaflets (Maya came with her, and they counted the number of houses where they could hear barking, which was quite a lot), that there would be phone calls and emails. Lots of calls would be nice, but she'd get at least one or two, surely?

50

But there weren't any, and Emily gloomily supposed that her leaflets had been thrown away, or maybe pinned up on a board like her mother's, just in case. It was very depressing, especially as Maya and the others kept asking if she'd heard anything and she had to say no.

At least she still had the shelter to go to. Maya and Emily arrived early on Saturday, and Lucy beamed at them.

"I'm really glad you two are here already! Twinkle's desperate for a walk. She's whining like mad. Some of the other volunteers have been taking the dogs out during the week, but I think she really loved those long walks she had last weekend." She eyed them hopefully. "Do you think you'd be up for taking two dogs each? If we make sure they're ones who'll get along?"

Emily glanced at Maya and they both nodded. "Definitely," Emily said. And Lucy was right – she could hear whining from the dog pens even out by the gate. She was pretty sure that Twinkle was making the squeaky, grumpy noise.

"You went towards the woods last week, didn't you," Lucy said thoughtfully as they got the dogs out. "Maybe today you could go across the fields, by the stream. I don't want you to get bored…"

"We won't," Emily giggled, as Twinkle bounced excitedly round her feet, and Trevor the Westie tied her up with his lead.

"Sammy wants to go now!" Maya said anxiously, gripping tightly on to the big black dog who was sniffing excitedly at everything he could reach, and pulling her step by step away from the dog pens. It didn't help that Barney was sitting down as usual, so she was being pulled in two different directions.

"Maybe you should tie their leads together," Emily suggested, as they headed out of the yard in the direction Lucy had pointed, down a little path to the fields. "Then Sammy could pull Barney along, and you'd just have to sort of point them in the right direction."

"They're trying to tear me in half," Maya grumbled, but she was laughing.

The dogs took up too much of the girls' attention for chatting, but by the time they were on their way back they'd worn off some of their energy, and it was a bit easier to talk.

"Lucy didn't say anything about the party, did she?" Maya said, side-stepping over Sammy's lead as he snapped at a butterfly in front of them.

PET PROTECTION

Emily shook her head. "Nooo… Maybe she thought we didn't really mean it. After all, we haven't come back with plans, have we?"

"It's a bit hard, when we can't think of anywhere to have it," Maya sighed. "Maybe we could just hope for the best and have it in the middle of the yard? The weather ought to be OK in June."

Emily shook her head. "No. My birthday's at the beginning of June too, which is nice because it's usually in the half-term holidays. But it's always, always raining on my birthday. Mum's stopped even suggesting outside parties. We need a hall or something. It would be really good if we found one with a garden, then we could do stuff outdoors if the weather actually is nice for once."

"I don't suppose school would let us use the hall…" Maya murmured.

"Not if we want to have the dogs and cats and guinea pigs around for people to meet," Emily pointed out. "I've been thinking about it. We can't really have a party for the shelter, and not have any of the animals there, can we? For a start because if they were there it would mean everybody met them. That would be a great way to find homes for some of them, don't you think?"

53

"Not Twinkle, though," Maya reminded her. "I know she's OK with you, but remember what Lucy said about her being jumpy and nervous?"

"I know. It would have to be just a few of the calmest, friendliest ones. Barney, for a start. Nothing upsets him. And maybe Whiskers, if he was only meeting people, and not other cats. Some guinea pigs? They're all friendly."

Maya started to laugh. "It probably isn't a good idea, but I just thought of the coolest party game. Pass the guinea pig. Whoever's got the guinea pig when the music stops gets a sweet."

Emily rolled her eyes. "And then the person left with the guinea pig after the last go takes it home? Yeah, I can definitely see Lucy agreeing to that." She sighed. "It would be fun though, wouldn't it? I bet we could think of some great things to do at the party. You know, that sort of thing but just a bit less mad. If we could only find somewhere."

"Are we going the right way?" Maya said suddenly. "I don't remember coming past this bit."

They were walking down a path at the edge of a field of long grass, with an old barn standing in the corner.

Emily frowned. "I think maybe we should have

gone the other way after we came over the little bridge. But I saw that barn earlier on, I'm sure I did. It's just that it was from the other side. I'm pretty sure we're still on the fields that belong to the shelter. We need to go across the other side of this field, and past the barn, I think. Then we should see the path back to the farmyard."

Maya shuddered. "I'm glad you know what you're doing. I'd be completely lost. I'm useless at directions."

They cut through the long grass – with Trevor bouncing up and down like a little white football so he could see where he was going – and went down the other side of the hedge instead, making for the barn.

"I wonder why they don't use this for any of the animal pens?" Emily said thoughtfully, as they got closer to it. "Maybe it isn't close enough to the yard."

"I think it's falling down." Maya shook her head. "I bet it would cost loads to make it into pens."

"Mmmm…" But Emily was frowning, as she walked closer. "Maybe. It doesn't look all that bad. The door's fallen off, that's all."

"Don't go *in* it!" Maya squeaked. "It might fall down on you!"

"Honestly, it's OK," Emily told her, peering through the open doorway. "And I'm not going right in, anyway, I'm not that stupid. We'd have to ask Lucy if it's safe." She gazed around, peering up at the dusty, cobwebby rafters. "I suppose it would be hard to turn it into part of the shelter. But there aren't any holes in the roof, I can see that from here. It's just a lovely, big, very, very dirty space…"

"Oh!" Maya came to look over her shoulder, and Sammy and Barney stuck their heads in and both sneezed loudly. "Oh, now I see what you mean! Well, you're right about it being dirty." She wrinkled her nose. "But I suppose it is big enough… And the field's beautiful."

"Exactly," Emily agreed. "And people could park in the lane outside the shelter, and walk through to here, so they'd see what they were raising money for!" She looked back at the huge, shadowy, dusty space, and then glanced anxiously at Maya. "Are we being stupid? Do you think we can actually turn this into a party room?"

Maya nodded slowly. "I reckon it's worth a try."

FIVE

"The old barn? Really?" Lucy stared at them doubtfully. "But it's just a shell…"

Emily nodded. "I know, but it's not falling down, is it? It's quite safe?"

"Well, yes… We had to have it checked out last year – to make sure it wasn't dangerous, in case anyone wandered into it and got hurt."

"Like you!" Maya nudged Emily.

"I was very careful." Emily rolled her eyes. "I know it looks a mess, but if we could clean it up, and decorate it, it would be great. You know, we'd put up balloons, and streamers and stuff. I bet we could make it look really special. And then we wouldn't have to pay for a party venue at all!"

"You might even be able to hire it out to other people for the same sort of thing," Maya suggested. "That would be a great way to raise money for the shelter."

Lucy raised her eyebrows. "Oh, wow. Yes... I hadn't thought of that. It does sound a really good idea ... but it's going to be a lot of work." She shook her head worriedly. "You two won't be able to do it on your own."

Maya and Emily grinned at her. "Don't worry, we won't have to. We've got some friends who'll help," Maya explained.

"Oooh! Do you think we could camp out in the barn for a weekend?" Emily asked excitedly. "Then we could make it a sort of weekend sleepover project. That would be excellent."

"Just you girls?" Lucy sounded a bit anxious, and Maya was shaking her head.

"Just us, in an old barn in the middle of a field? That would be too spooky, Ems..."

Emily twirled a finger in her curls and frowned. "I suppose it might be. But what about if I could get my mum to come as well? Then it wouldn't be scary, would it?"

Maya nodded. "That would be OK. I think. But your mum wouldn't, would she? You always say she's so busy with Sukie and the boys."

"I know," Emily agreed. "But she *really* loves

58

camping. It's her favourite thing. She and my dad used to go on backpacking holidays before she had us, and she took me and Toby camping lots when we were little. She's been saying that she'd love to do it again, but it's harder with four kids, that's all. If I got my dad to say he'd look after Toby and James and Sukie, Mum could have a girls' sleepover with us. I bet she'd love it." *I'd love it*, Emily added silently.

It would be amazing to have Mum to herself for once. And her mum had been really enthusiastic about Emily helping at the shelter. Emily was sure that she'd like to help out somehow too.

The girls peeped into the barn again on their second walk of the day. It was definitely going to be a lot of work to clear it all out, but it was such a lovely big space – loads of room for all sorts of crazy games!

Emily hurried back home feeling excited about the party all over again – it was beginning to look as though it would actually happen!

She bounced into the house eager to tell everyone the news and ask Mum if she fancied a special weekend camp-out. As she shut the door, she could hear the phone ringing, and Mum yelled down the stairs: "Can one of you answer that, please!

I'm changing Sukie."

Emily was just hurrying into the kitchen to grab the phone when Toby snatched it up, grinning at her triumphantly. He loved answering the phone, but he was only five, and he wasn't always great at passing on messages, so Emily hovered by the door, ready to help him out. She could hear the person on the other end of the phone talking, and Toby was scowling, as though he didn't understand what they were saying.

"What's the matter? Who is it?" she whispered. But Toby glared at her. It was his phone, and he wasn't giving it up.

"It's for Mum," he hissed, shoving past her out of the door, and Emily sighed. It probably was, but if she'd answered it, she would have said to call back. Mum wouldn't want to talk right now.

She followed Toby up the stairs, hoping that the phone call wouldn't leave Mum feeling harassed. She wanted to be able to talk to her about sleepovers in tatty old barns, and it was going to need Mum to be in a good mood. A really good mood.

Mum was sticking Sukie's nappy together with one hand while she tucked the phone under her chin with the other. "Mmmm, yes. Emily does live here. I'm sorry, that was my little boy, he can't have understood. Er – you want to talk to Emily?" Mum frowned. "About *what*, sorry?" She turned round and raised one eyebrow at Emily – it was a knack she had, Emily wished she could do it too. With Mum it always meant, *what on earth have you done now*?

"Mrs Everett, could Emily please call you back in five minutes? Would that be all right?" She made frantic "pen" signals at Emily, and Sukie's nappy fell off.

Emily sighed, grabbed one of Sukie's crayons, and scribbled down the number.

"Five minutes! Thanks so much!" Her mum handed the phone to Toby, whisked Sukie's nappy back on, and even managed to get a pair of trousers over the top before Sukie noticed. Then she glared at Emily. "Mrs Everett, Emily sweetness, appears to think that we are running a dog-walking business. She would like us to walk her cocker spaniel, Charlie, three times a week. And she thinks our rates sound very reasonable."

"Really?" Emily squeaked excitedly. "She actually wants me to walk a dog? Oh, wow!"

"Emily Laura Harris!" her mum snapped. "Why is this lady calling us about spaniels? Since when do you walk dogs?"

"Ummmm…" Emily smiled at her hopefully. "It was Poppy's idea. To start a dog-walking business. I was saying how lucky she was having Billy, and I said I wished I had a dog like him—"

Her mum rolled her eyes. "I don't. That dog is a nightmare!"

"He's ever so sweet though, isn't he? I know he's messy, but he's very friendly. But I know we can't," Emily added hurriedly. "I was explaining to the others about there being too many of us in the house already, and how we couldn't fit in a dog." She sighed, very quietly. "Anyway. That was when Izzy suggested helping at the shelter – and Poppy had the idea about the dog-walking too."

Her mum was putting away the nappy-changing stuff, rather slowly, and not really looking at her. "I didn't know you were still thinking about it…" she murmured. "I knew you were excited about the shelter, but I hadn't realised… It was such a long time ago that we had that talk."

Emily shrugged uncomfortably. "I know – I'd still love to have a pet of our own, though. I mean, don't worry, I know we can't. That's why Izzy and Poppy had such brilliant ideas. They were ways I could almost have my own dog, without us having a dog in the house to make more stress for you and Dad. You see?"

Her mum nodded slowly, and put a wooden puzzle down in front of Sukie to stop her trying to play with the nappy cream. Then she looked up at Emily, frowning. "But how did this Mrs Everett get our number?"

Emily swallowed, suddenly realising that her parents might not be that happy about leaflets with their phone number on being in houses all round Appleby. They also weren't going to be that keen on her wandering around the village on her own either, she suspected. (Well, with a dog, but she had a feeling her mum was going to say that didn't count. She and Poppy and the others hadn't really got as far as thinking about that…)

"I made a leaflet," she said, crossing her fingers behind her back. "I delivered them to all the houses round us. Houses that are close enough for me to walk to, so I'd be able to go and pick up their dogs. I only printed fifty, but they went quite a long way. I didn't bother putting them through the door at houses where I knew there wasn't a dog."

"When?" her mother demanded, her eyes wide. "I didn't see you delivering any leaflets!"

"Before school one day. I got up really early and nipped out." She smiled shyly at her mum – who wasn't shouting yet, which was a good sign. "It was really exciting. But then nobody called for ages, and I almost forgot about it. I just supposed nobody round here needed a dog-walker."

"I think Mrs Everett must be quite elderly," her mum said thoughtfully. "If she's who I think she is, she lives in that tiny cottage with the green window frames, and the painted mushrooms in the garden. You know, the one James used to make us stop at every time we went past, so we could count them."

"Oh!" Emily smiled. She loved those mushrooms too. Mrs Everett must be nice, if she lived there, she thought. "So maybe she needs help giving her dog enough walks, then."

"Mmmmm." Her mum stared at her, frowning thoughtfully, and Emily looked back. She had absolutely no idea what her mum was going to say. She couldn't even tell if she was cross or not.

"I'm really not very happy with you," her mum said, even though she didn't actually sound very cross.

Emily sighed. That answered that then.

"You shouldn't have done all this without asking.

You're already helping at the shelter, isn't that enough?"

"I suppose so," Emily said sadly. "It's just – all those dogs are going to have new homes, or we hope they are. I'll never be able to look after any of them for very long. I was thinking that if I walked the same dog every week, it would be like it was mine? Just a little bit?"

"Oh, Emily." Her mum put an arm round her shoulders, and Sukie giggled and flung herself at their knees, thinking it was a group hug.

Emily crouched down and cuddled her little sister. However much she envied Sukie sometimes, getting all Mum's attention, she *was* cute, and very cuddly when she felt like it.

"I didn't realise how much you were still wishing we could get a dog," her mum sighed.

Emily glanced up at her hopefully. That didn't sound like *No, of course you can't go off walking other people's dogs round the village on your own*, which was what she'd been expecting her mum to say.

"Will you be able to fit walking another dog in, if you're helping at the shelter as well?" her mum asked. "Don't forget you've got dancing on Mondays as well. And twice a week when there's a show coming up, or the dance exams."

"You mean I can do it!" Emily yelped excitedly, almost tipping Sukie over.

Sukie smacked her in the leg with the puzzle, and stomped out of the room muttering. Mum had to chase after her.

"Yes," she called back up the stairs. "But only if I get to speak to your customers first, do you understand? You'd better ring that lady back. And be polite, Emily! Don't forget to write down everything, so you know what time she wants you to come, all that sort of thing."

"I will! I promise!" Emily grabbed the piece of paper with the crayon scribble, and dialled the number with shaky fingers.

◆

"He's a very good dog usually," Mrs Everett said, pushing the plate of biscuits across the table to Emily. "But he's an absolute terror if he sees a cat, I'm afraid. I never could train him out of it." She looked worriedly at Emily. "Do you think you'll be able to cope? I hadn't realised quite how young you were…"

Emily took a deep breath. She'd had a feeling Mrs Everett was going to say something like this, ever since the old lady had opened the front door. She'd suggested yesterday on the phone that Emily should come round for a cup of tea to discuss the times for walking Charlie, and Emily had said it would have to be after school. But Mrs Everett had probably thought she was a teenager.

"I know I'm young, but I'm good with dogs, I really am," she promised, gripping the table leg so she was touching wood for luck, and crossing the fingers of her other hand. "I help out at Appleby Animal Rescue, and I walk lots of dogs there. Even ones that are quite nervous, and need, um, careful handling."

"Oh." Mrs Everett nodded thoughtfully. "Well. I suppose you could try, anyway. I must say, I'm very impressed with your initiative, even if you are young. And Charlie seems to like you." She smiled at the little reddish-brown spaniel, who was sitting with his nose on Emily's leg, gazing up at her adoringly.

"To be honest, that's probably because he thinks I'm going to give him a biscuit," Emily admitted. "But I wouldn't!" she added hurriedly. "Especially not these chocolate ones."

"Why not chocolate ones?" Mrs Everett frowned at her, looking confused. "Because they're more fattening?"

"Oh! No, it's something I read in a dog magazine," Emily explained shyly. "I don't actually have my own dog, but I've always liked getting the magazine anyway. I cut the pictures out." She flushed pink, realising this sounded a bit silly. "Um. It was at Christmas and there was a special article saying make sure you don't put boxes of chocolates under the tree as a present for someone, in case your dog eats them. Chocolate's poisonous to dogs. Mostly it's dark chocolate that's the problem, and they have to eat quite a bit of it, but they could even die, if they eat enough. There's a chemical in chocolate, I think it's called theobromine. Something like that. But it still tastes yummy to them, so they eat it anyway even though it's so dangerous."

"Good gracious!" Mrs Everett looked at the biscuits in horror. "I never knew that. I'm sure Charlie's had the odd chocolate biscuit when I'm not looking."

"I shouldn't think there's enough chocolate on them to hurt him," Emily said reassuringly. She really hadn't meant to upset the old lady, but Mrs Everett looked quite impressed, as though Emily was some sort of dog expert.

Charlie stared up at her with reproachful, almond-shaped dark eyes. Clearly he suspected that there wouldn't be any more sneaky chocolate biscuits, and it was all Emily's fault. She rubbed his ears apologetically.

"How often would you like me to take him out?" she asked.

"Well, could you fit in three walks a week?" Mrs Everett asked. "I can take him for a short walk every day, and he has the garden, but I just can't manage the nice long walks he really loves. I've got a problem with one of my knees, you see."

"That would be great," Emily said enthusiastically. "I could take him along by the stream, maybe. Or across the common."

Mrs Everett sighed. "Yes, he loves it there, sniffing all the rabbit holes. But that's just a bit too far for me now, except on a very good day. I can tell he's going to have a lovely time with you." She smiled, and reached down to stroke Charlie's silky domed head. "I really am so glad I called you, Emily."

Emily beamed back at her. "I'm ever so glad too. I can't wait to start walking him!"

SIX

"We're nearly home now," Emily told Charlie. He was dragging his paws a bit, and she looked down at him anxiously. He'd had loads of energy when they first set off, so they'd gone quite a long way – but that meant they had to come quite a long way back again, and the little spaniel was definitely tired.

"I hope Mrs Everett isn't going to be upset that I wore you out," Emily muttered. "I didn't mean to… Do you want a carry, Charlie?" That was what they did with Sukie, when she started sitting down and sulking, and they didn't have the pushchair. Emily crouched down and looked at Charlie, and he gazed back at her, with his tongue hanging out.

"I reckon I can carry you for the last five minutes. Poor baby. Carry, yes? Is that OK?" She picked him up carefully, cradling him in her arms. "Wow. You're a lot heavier than you look, Charlie.

PET PROTECTION

Too many biscuits."

Emily and Charlie staggered back along Mrs Everett's road, and Charlie wriggled out of her arms when he saw his front gate, and dragged Emily up the path with a sudden burst of energy.

"Oh, *now* you're all bouncy…" Emily muttered. "I think my arms are going to fall off."

"It looks like he had a lovely time!" Mrs Everett laughed, opening her front door, and sidestepping as Charlie shot inside. "Goodness, where are you going?"

"He probably wants a drink of water," Emily explained apologetically. "We went quite a long way, and he got worn out by the end of it. I carried him the last little bit – he just suddenly went all tired and feeble. Sorry…"

"Oh, but that's good!" Mrs Everett assured her. "He hardly ever gets a good long walk like that now, and he is getting a little bit of a tummy. I'm sure he'll get used to proper walks again in no time." She sighed. "I just wish that I could take him myself."

Emily nodded. She didn't really know what to say – it must be so sad for Mrs Everett. It sounded like she'd loved taking Charlie out, before her knee got so bad, and she'd told Emily about all the different dogs she'd owned over the years. She'd always had dogs around, and now she was feeling that she couldn't look after Charlie properly.

Mrs Everett smiled at her. "Don't worry, Emily, honestly. It's lovely to know that he's going to get proper walks. You're a star. And I'll tell your mum that, as well. I saw her and your gorgeous little sister in the shop this morning, and she did look a bit worried about your business venture. But I think you're very clever."

"It was my friend's idea," Emily explained rather shyly. "Mum and Dad love dogs, but there's me and Sukie and my two brothers. They think a dog would be too much."

Mrs Everett nodded. "Oh, well, it depends on the dog, doesn't it? With that many people in the house already, you'd need a really nicely trained dog. Maybe not a puppy, they can be silly round small children."

"I know." Emily nodded. "I think we'd be all right – but it's not up to me…" She sighed, and then grinned at the old lady. "But now I get to walk Charlie. I don't think I'm very good at being in business, you know. I'd walk him for free."

"You will not!" Mrs Everett gave her a pretend-fierce look. "I'll pay you at the end of the week. And

PET PROTECTION

I'll tell any of my friends who might need a bit of dog-walking help, if you like. You could fit a couple more dogs in, don't you think?"

Emily nodded. "Yes, please!" She leaned close to Mrs Everett to whisper. "I'm saving up to have my own dog, you see. One day I will."

◆

"This weekend's going to be so exciting!" Maya leaned over Izzy's shoulder. "What's that a list of?"

"Stuff we need to bring." Izzy frowned thoughtfully across the playground. "Sleeping bags. Camping mats to lie on. What's the floor made out of, Emily? Is it muddy?"

"Ummm, well, it's mud, but it's not muddy, if you see what I mean." Emily frowned. "Dry mud."

Izzy wrinkled her nose and wrote down *groundsheets*.

"My mum said we maybe ought to bring our tent," Emily said, looking at the list.

"But I thought we were sleeping in the barn?" Maya looked confused.

"Mmmm. But Dad pointed out it's probably going to be really cold in such a big space. Especially as we'll be sleeping on the floor. We've got a sort of pop-up tent, one that doesn't need much pegging out – it would be tricky to bang the pegs in, because the floor's all trodden down and hard, you see. It would just be like a little bedroom inside the barn."

Maya nodded. "I guess you're the expert."

Emily grinned at her. "It's ages since I've been camping, though. I'm really looking forward to it."

"You know what I'm not looking forward to?" Izzy said worriedly. "If we have to go to the loo in the middle of the night. I know you said the lady from the shelter's letting us use her loo, but I don't want to walk across two fields in the dark!"

"You won't have to, though. We've got one of those bucket loos. Camping ones," Emily pointed out.

Izzy shuddered. "Actually, that sounds worse."

"You could always nip behind a tree!" Maya giggled.

"Yes, but other things might be behind it with me," said Izzy with a shiver. "You know. Foxes. Or a badger."

"Maybe even a wolf," Emily said, straight-faced, and Izzy stared at her in horror.

"Not really? But I thought they were only in Scotland? Oh! You're having me on."

"Of course I am! There aren't wild wolves

anywhere in Britain now!" Emily shook her head, giggling.

Izzy sighed. "You're so mean. I can't help it, I kind of like my nice warm bathroom. And loo paper."

"Put loo paper on the list," Emily told her. "The nice quilted stuff."

✦

"Wow…" Poppy spun round slowly, staring up at the dusty rafters and the stained, dirty plaster on the walls.

Emily made a face. "I know. It's a mess. Maybe this wasn't a good idea."

But Poppy shook her head. "Oh no, I didn't mean that! It's amazing. Those wooden beam things, it's beautiful."

"You think so?" Emily asked hopefully, looking round at all the others. "It's just it looks like such a lot of work – I think I'd deliberately forgotten how bad it was, and then we walked in and I suddenly remembered…" She gazed helplessly at the dusty floor, which was covered in sticks, and bits of rubbish, and something that looked like it might be a dead mouse.

"My mum and dad got married in a place that looked a lot like this," Maya said. "I've seen the photos

– I was only about three, so I don't really remember it. But it was beautiful. There were loads of flowers everywhere, like long ropes of flowers hanging off the rafters."

"We can't do that." Izzy shook her head firmly. "Too expensive."

"Goodness." Emily's mum walked into the barn – she hadn't run across the field like the girls, mostly because she was carrying a tent, and had sleeping bags dangling off all her fingers.

"What do you think?" Emily asked her anxiously, hurrying over to help her put the tent down.

Her mum looked around with half-closed eyes, and then smiled at her. "I think you two were very clever to spot it. But has Lucy got a ladder? I can't see anyone having a party in here with all those spider webs hanging down. It's making me quivery just looking at them. Can we get rid of them first?"

Poppy nodded. "I should have brought Billy. He loves hunting spiders. I don't think he ever actually catches them, he just runs along behind them making these big snapping noises."

"Oh, Henry catches them." Maya shuddered. "And then he eats them, it's disgusting. Actually, it might not be a bad idea to bring him along. I bet there's mice in here." She crouched down by the tiny little morsel of fur that Emily had spotted in one corner. "Yup, definitely. Henry's a fab mouser."

"But if it's a party all about raising money for rescuing animals and looking after them…" Emily began.

"Ems, I don't think that goes as far as mice," her mum said gently. "Especially not if you're having food at this party. Do you want to get the tent up?"

Emily sighed. "I suppose so. It feels mean to the mice, that's all."

"They can all move back in after the party," Maya said, hugging her. "Henry's just going to persuade them to go on a camping holiday for a bit. Like us."

✦

"It's really odd not being able to hear any cars," Poppy murmured.

"Mmmm…" Izzy agreed sleepily.

"Sounds just like it does at home to me," Maya yawned. "Except usually I've got Henry snoring at the end of my bed."

"Me too!" Emily whispered back. "Sukie snores, and so does my dad. Like a jet engine or something."

"Is your mum asleep?" Maya whispered.

"Probably." Emily sat up a bit and listened. Their

tent had two bedrooms, and it was meant to sleep three people in each, but the girls had decided they'd all squash into one of them, and leave the other one for Emily's mum and all their bags. Emily's mum had pretended to be hurt, but she didn't really mind. Emily had checked. Mum had said that as long as they didn't wake her up because they needed a drink, or they wanted to go to the loo, or they felt sick, or they'd had a bad dream about the whole family being eaten by velociraptors, she really didn't care who slept where, and Emily was pretty sure she meant it.

"Do you think all those spiders went out of the door in the end?" Izzy murmured.

"Yes," Maya said firmly. "Especially after Emily chased that big one out with the broom."

"It was massive." Poppy shuddered.

"Oy! We all shake about when you wriggle like that! Izzy nearly put her foot up my nose," Emily protested. They were all squashed up sharing the sleeping pod, but at least it was really cosy.

Maya sniggered. "If I have to get up to go to the loo, I'll have to walk on you, you know that, don't you." She yawned massively. "I was going to say we ought to stay up till midnight at least, but I'm really sleepy. All that sweeping the floor wore me out."

PET PROTECTION

"And we've got to do painting tomorrow, that's even harder," Poppy murmured from the other end of the pod. "It wears your arms out. Doesn't it, Izzy? You did your room with your dad, didn't you?"

There was a short silence, and then Emily giggled. "I think she's asleep."

No one answered, and she sighed. "They're all asleep. Wusses." She rolled over, and nudged Izzy's feet out of the way of her pillow. "Night, then…"

✦

"It was such a good idea bringing the camping stove." Emily sniffed, and sighed happily as the steam from the hot-chocolate pan wafted up her nose. "It was worth lugging all those water carriers and things over from the car, Mum."

"There's something about sleeping outside – or almost outside – that makes everyone starving." Her mum poured hot chocolate into five mugs. "I knew you'd want something hot for breakfast, even though you swore to me you all wanted Coco Pops."

"This is really nice," Emily sighed. The others were still asleep – or only awake as far as the groaning and wriggling stage anyway. But she had a feeling the hot-chocolate smell would bring them out of the tent soon. She looked thoughtfully at the big pile of supplies she and her mum had packed – big water carriers, a packet of cereal, a cool box with milk and all the stuff for sandwiches. "We're going to have to bring *everything* for the party out here too. Water for squash. All the food. It's going to be tricky remembering all of it."

Her mum grinned. "Oh, you'll be fine. You've got Izzy and her amazing list."

Emily nodded. "We need to start writing down ideas for what we're actually doing at the party today. But we can talk about that while we're painting." She gazed around the barn. "It already looks loads better with the floor all swept." Then she frowned, putting her head on one side. "What's that funny noise? It sounds like a motorbike or something."

Emily got up, and hopped carefully across the barn floor with her feet half in her wellies. "Oh! Hello!"

"Who is it?" her mum called anxiously. They hadn't expected any visitors.

"It's Izzy's dad! And his lawnmower! Izzy!" Emily yelled over the noise of the ride-on mower.

There was a sudden silence as Izzy's dad turned the mower off, and Izzy poked her face out of the tent, blinking sleepily.

"Your dad's here!" Emily told her, and she

80

squeaked, and dived back into the tent to put her glasses on.

"She's not even up?" Her dad shook his head, pretending to be horrified. "Typical. Sorry to turn up so early, Emily. Iz mentioned that you were thinking of using the field for games and things, so I thought I could come and cut the grass for you. I've got a job later on, so I was fitting you in before." He looked around at the barn. "This is a beautiful old place." Then he frowned at the battered doors. "All your work tidying it up's going to be wasted though, if you can't shut these doors. The grot's just going to blow back in."

Emily came to look at them with him. "I know, but they're really wobbly. I tried closing them, and I thought they were going to fall apart on top of me."

"Mmmm." Mr Armstrong frowned. "I've got some bits of wood I can mend those with, I reckon. The frame looks all right."

"Really?" Emily felt like hugging him, but Izzy beat her to it. She came dashing across the barn in just her pyjamas and socks, and flung her arms round her dad.

"Thanks, Dad! I did wonder if you could, but it felt a bit mean asking when you said you were really busy this weekend."

Her dad shrugged. "Well. You did say the shelter badly needs the money. And it's sad seeing a lovely old place like this falling apart." He peered at the doors, and frowned. "After I've been to the Johnsons' this morning I'll nip home and find the wood for you."

By now the other two were wriggling out of the tent door, yawning and blinking owlishly.

"Uuurrrh, it's chilly," Poppy muttered, and Emily handed her a mug of hot chocolate. Poppy woke up a bit after she'd had a couple of mouthfuls, and eyed Izzy's dad.

"Hi, Mr Armstrong…" she said, sounding confused, and obviously wondering why he was there, and whether she'd missed something.

"He's come to cut the grass," Emily explained, taking pity on her. "And hopefully mend the doors too."

"If the grass is all cut," Izzy said, as she dived back into the tent again to put her clothes on, "we need to think about how we're going to use all that big space outside." The next bit was totally muffled, and Emily guessed she was pulling her sweater over her head and still talking.

PET PROTECTION

"What did you say?" she asked, as Izzy came out again, looking worryingly awake and organised. She was even holding a pen.

"Games!" Izzy said briskly, pulling her notebook out of her pocket. "What are we going to do?"

"I'm not awake yet," Maya moaned. "It isn't even eight o'clock. I can't *think*."

Emily grinned at her mum. "It's like a lie-in, not getting up till now. Sukie usually wakes up at about half-past five and yells till everyone else wakes up too. I wonder how Dad's doing…"

Her mum sighed happily. "It does seem very peaceful. Eat some cereal, you lot. Maybe that'll wake you all up. Have you had breakfast?" she asked Izzy's dad, waving a bowl at him.

"I could have a second breakfast… Izzy never lets me have these," her dad explained, pouring himself the chocolatey cereal. "She says they're bad for us."

Izzy went pink, and Emily's mum laughed as she handed the bowls around. "Don't worry, Izzy, I totally agree with you. But you've never been shopping with Emily and Toby and James. I come home with stuff I never intended to buy at all. Especially now we do the self-scanning thing. James bought smoked salmon last week. He doesn't even like it, and it was *very* expensive. Sukie's even worse, she just chucks everything in the trolley without scanning it, and then the people at the checkout think we're trying to shoplift... Anyway, I think chocolate cereal's OK for weekends. And especially for camping. We always have treats then."

"What games are we going to have at the party?" Izzy said, changing the subject, and balancing her notebook on her knee behind the bowl.

"I still like the idea of pass the guinea pig," Maya sighed, scooping the last of her cereal into her mouth. "I love them so much – the way they squeak, and they always look so surprised."

"You could adopt one from the shelter," Poppy pointed out, and Maya looked at her in surprise.

"I s'pose I could. I hadn't thought of it. I reckon Henry might think it was breakfast on legs, though."

Emily snorted. "I don't know. Some of those guinea pigs at the shelter are massive. I think they could take Henry, no problem. Especially if you had two of them."

Maya smiled to herself. "It *is* nearly my birthday. And Mum was saying she hadn't got a clue what to get me."

Emily nodded, swallowing a little. She wished it

was that easy. She stared down at her bowl, very carefully not looking at her mum.

Poppy was chewing the end of her spoon, and scowling. "Maybe… Hmmmm… It would be good if we did stuff that made people think about the shelter, wouldn't it? And if the grass is cut outside, there'll be loads of room. As long as it's not raining. Why don't we have a dog show?"

Emily widened her eyes. "Isn't that a bit complicated? I mean, you have to know all about the different breeds, it's really tricky. I mean, I know some, but I couldn't tell you what colour eyes a Lhasa Apso's supposed to have, or anything like that."

"A whatter whatter?" Maya asked.

Emily shrugged. "Mad hairy thing. But really cute. You see? No way we can judge a dog show."

"I don't mean that sort of dog show!" Poppy shook her head. "I mean a *fun* dog show. Waggiest tail. Dog that looks most like its owner. Oooooh! Dog fancy dress! OK, someone else has to be in charge – I need to enter Billy."

Izzy was scribbling frantically, and everyone was nodding.

"Very good idea," Emily's mum agreed. "And if you charge a little bit to enter each class – a pound maybe – then that raises you even more money. I'm sure I could find you some rosettes on the Internet, and perhaps you could give some dog treats for the first prize as well."

The girls packed the breakfast things into a bowl to wash up later, still talking excitedly about different dog show ideas. Emily's mum got out the tins of white paint that Emily's dad had found at the back of their garage, and Emily handed round a pile of ancient shirts.

"I've never done this before," Maya murmured, looking at the walls rather anxiously.

"It's OK," Emily assured her. "It's not difficult. You just splash it on – I mean, there's no radiators to go round, or worrying about not getting it on the carpet. Just go for it."

"However bad we are, it's still going to look loads better," Poppy agreed, loading up her brush, and slapping a big stroke of white paint across the dirty plaster. "Look! It looks fab! Actually, it would be really nice to draw on…" She half closed her eyes, looking around as if she could see the walls covered in glittering colour.

"No!" Emily pushed Poppy's brush back against the wall. "At least, not until we've painted everything

PET PROTECTION

white. Then we'll think about it!"

✦

"Hey! Look at this!" Izzy's dad stood in the doorway, staring round admiringly. "It looks amazing – it's bigger!"

"It does look bigger," Emily agreed. "It's the white, I suppose. We're almost done. Just this little bit. And guess what we found!"

Izzy grabbed her dad's hand, and pulled him over to the darkest corner.

"An old tin bath!" He laughed. "Maybe someone was using it to feed the animals from. Or they just put all their old bits of rubbish in the barn. You were lucky the whole place wasn't filled up with junk." He walked round it, rubbing his chin. "Just a couple of holes in it… It would be brilliant in a garden, you know. Imagine it all full of tulips." He put on a very serious face. "Miss Harris, Miss Armstrong, could I make you an offer for this beautiful bath? Ten pounds to the party fund? Actually, I tell you what – how about I buy it off you, but I'll plant it up and leave it here until after the party?"

Emily blinked. "I was going to get Mum to take it home with us and take it to the tip!" she said, giggling. "Yes, please buy it! It'll look really nice with flowers in – like the barn's got people here all the time."

"Someone's coming with a dog," Poppy called from the top of the stepladder. "I can hear barking."

"Oh, maybe it's Lucy," Emily said, hurrying over to look. "She said she'd come if there weren't too many people looking round the shelter this afternoon." Then she squeaked delightedly. "Mrs Everett! And you've got Charlie. Mum, look, I know you've met Mrs Everett, but this is her gorgeous dog that I've been walking." She made a fuss of Charlie, tickling him under the chin until he rolled over and waved his paws in the air.

Her mum laughed and crouched down to stroke him. "He's lovely. You know, your dad had a dog really like Charlie when we first met. He was called Tigger because he bounced everywhere."

Emily nodded. "Charlie's a bit bouncy when he's about to go for a walk, but most of the time he's a little star. Aren't you?"

Charlie wriggled the right way up, and did his angelic melting-eyed look at Emily's mum, resting his chin on her knees and staring up at her soulfully.

Emily looked up anxiously at Mrs Everett. "I've just thought. You've come a long way. Are you... I mean, is your leg all right?"

PET PROTECTION

Mrs Everett smiled at her, and sighed. "I might sit down on that bit of wall over there for a bit, Emily. I'm having a good day, and it's been a lovely walk, but it's a bit far for me now, to be honest. But haven't you made the old barn look nice? Cutting the grass has made a huge difference. And the paint! How's the planning coming along?"

Emily had told Mrs Everett all about the rescue centre, and the party. Mrs Everett always invited her in after she'd walked Charlie, and she was nice to talk to. She'd had some good ideas for the party already. Emily's favourite was a craft table for everyone to make animal hats to dress up in.

"We're going to have a dog show. Oh! You could enter Charlie, he'd win waggiest tail, no problem. Actually— " Emily looked hopeful. "Would you like to be a judge instead? You'd be really good at it!"

"Oh, yes." Poppy nodded, peering down from the ladder. "You, and Lucy from the rescue centre. That would be great."

"I'd love to." Mrs Everett smiled at them all. "I was trying to think of a way I could help you all. Oooh, I'm looking forward to this party now, girls. You'd better decide on a date and get those tickets out there, hadn't you?"

SEVEN

Emily and Maya checked with Lucy about the date for the party when she came to see how they were doing later on. She was amazed at how good they'd made the barn look.

"I wish we'd thought about doing something like this ages ago," she murmured, wandering around the barn as they told her all their plans.

"We need you to help us choose when to have the party," Emily explained. "It would be great if you could help with the dog-show judging – you know loads about dogs. And we'll need to make sure there's lots of volunteers at the shelter on the day too, to show people around."

They were all really hoping that some party guests would fall in love with the cats and dogs they saw, and that lots of the pets would end up being rehomed.

"Do you think we can still have the party in half-term?" Izzy suggested. "That's what you said first of all, wasn't it? Do you think we can be ready in time? It's only three weeks from now. Four weeks if we made the party on the second Saturday. And that's the first of June, so it'll be an easy date for people to remember, too."

Lucy nodded. "That sounds good to me. I'll let all the volunteers know that it would be great if they could help out then."

"And they get to come to the party as well," Emily added quickly. "Just not all at the same time."

Izzy looked down at her notes worriedly. "I really hope it doesn't rain. I know we wanted the barn so things can be inside if it does, but it would be hard to squash a dog show in here too."

Poppy nodded. "I know, and that bit does sound like it's going to be really fun." She looked modestly down at her feet, and then snorted with laughter as Emily elbowed her in the ribs.

"What are you going to dress Billy up as?" Maya asked

"I honestly don't know." Poppy frowned. "It would be good to find something he looks a bit like anyway... A little boy did once ask his mum if Billy was an anteater when we were in the park. But I'm not sure how I'd make an anteater costume. Actually I'm not sure how I'd get Billy to keep any sort of costume on for more than ten seconds."

"Why an anteater?" Emily asked. "He doesn't look like an anteater!"

Poppy shrugged. "Well, I don't think he does. But it was his long nose, I guess. I wonder if I could make him a dinosaur costume? Billy the T-rex?"

"I wish we could enter cats as well," Maya said. "But I suppose it would be a disaster. I just like the idea of dressing Henry up."

Emily raised her eyebrows. "Maya, I've met your cat. He'd have your hand off if you tried to dress him up."

Maya sighed. "Probably. He isn't talking to me at the moment, anyway. It's because I was trying to get him to eat vegetarian cat food again. I tried ages ago, but I got it out again the other day, just to see if he'd changed his mind. Like people are supposed to have to try new foods seventeen times and then they get used to the taste."

"I suppose he still didn't like it?" Lucy asked, laughing.

"No. He just sniffed at it, then he went out and caught a mouse. I'm not sure if he was trying to tell me something, or if it was just a coincidence, but he did give me a really dirty look. And then he let the mouse go in the kitchen, and it got under the dishwasher. Anna blamed me, as well!"

"He *is* descended from tigers, Maya," Emily pointed out. "He probably thinks vegetarian cat food is an insult."

"It's very expensive!" Maya protested. "But he just likes tins. Or catching his own." She grinned to herself. "If I did dress him up, I think I'd dress him as a dog, just to be really mean. Oooh, Poppy, he could be a double act with Billy. You could make Billy a cat!"

Poppy rolled her eyes. "He'd probably try to chase himself."

"Maybe I could enter one of the dogs from the shelter?" Emily said thoughtfully, but then she saw Lucy's doubtful face. "No, I suppose not. They might be a bit too nervous for something like that." She sighed quietly. Mrs Everett would probably have let her enter Charlie, but it wouldn't be fair, when she was one of the judges!

It would have been so much fun to enter her own dog in the show, that was all.

✦

"I emailed the man at the newspaper," Izzy told Emily at school later that week. "I told him about the party, and I attached the information you sent about the shelter, and the photos of Twinkle, and Honey and the puppies, and that gorgeous white cat. I said people could ring up the shelter and book their tickets, and then pay on the day. That's right, isn't it?"

Emily nodded. "I can't think of a better way. We can't really give out our phone numbers when we're going to be at school all day."

"I really hope they put it in the paper," Izzy said. "We've put lots of posters up, but everyone gets that paper through their door, so it would make a big difference. I emailed the local radio people too, and the TV news programme – the ones who came to film the fashion show. I hope Lucy doesn't mind, because I said they could call the shelter as well, if they wanted to go and film there."

"She'd love it," Emily said. "Well, she would if they told her before they were coming so she didn't have her worst jeans on, anyway. Think how many extra people would go to the shelter, or even just give them some money, if it was on TV." She grinned. "And imagine how cute Posy would be. And the puppies! Still, even if it doesn't get on the news, I'm sure people will know about it. I went to walk Charlie last night, and Mrs Everett told me she went into town with her daughter to go shopping, and she saw four posters for the party! So we must have done something right."

✦

"Hi, Emily! Hi, Maya!" Lucy popped her head round the door to the cats' area and waved. "If I were you, I wouldn't go anywhere near Sal in the office. She says she's done nothing but answer the phone to people wanting party tickets this week. She doesn't usually come in on a Saturday, but she said she'd have to so as to catch up with all the other stuff she should have been doing."

"Really?" Emily squeaked excitedly. "Have lots of people asked for tickets then? How many are coming?"

"More than a hundred already," Lucy told her, laughing at Emily's half-horrified, half-excited face. "And you've got eleven entries for the dog fancy dress, six for the dog who looks most like their owner, and ten for waggiest tail!"

"But that's twenty-seven pounds just from the dog show bit!" Emily gasped, and Maya grabbed her hands and they started to dance madly around the yard.

"I'm really glad my mum said she'd help with the food," Emily said, panting, as they slowed down and staggered dizzily back towards Lucy. "More than a hundred people?"

"And that's only after a week," Lucy pointed out. "There's another two weeks till the party. It could be lots more." She put an arm round each of them. "I actually think you girls are going to raise enough money to get the roof mended, do you realise? The newspaper article was amazing – a couple of people have sent us cheques already, you know! There was one old gentleman who said he was probably a bit old for a party, but he really wanted to help."

Emily nodded. "It was a lovely piece – a whole page, and they put all the photos in."

"Do you want to hear the absolute best thing?" Lucy said, beaming. "A lady rang up yesterday to say that Posy was gorgeous, and her family loved Jack Russells, and could they come and meet her. They're coming today."

"Yeeeess!" Emily hugged her. "Oh, can we go and brush Posy? Or give her a bath, maybe?"

Maya grabbed her hand. "It might be too late.

Look, there's a car pulling up. It could be them already."

Emily looked anxiously over at the car, and the people getting out of it. Posy was really cute – she was quite stubborn, but Lucy said all Jack Russells were like that. And if these people loved Jack Russells, perhaps they wouldn't mind.

"I want to listen to what they say about her!" Maya whispered. "I hope they're nice. I want her to live somewhere lovely."

Emily nodded. She wanted fabulous homes for all the dogs, especially Barney, because he was so funny, and she knew it was going to be hard to find owners for such an old dog. And then there was her favourite dog at the shelter, Twinkle the whippet. Twinkle needed someone really gentle. They all needed special people, that was the problem.

"Could you take Spike and Twinkle out for me, girls?" Lucy asked, as she hurried over towards the gate. "And Lulu and Sam, if you can manage two each?"

"Course," Emily said eagerly. "Be slow putting their leads on," she added to Maya in a whisper, and Maya nodded. They strolled over towards the pens, eavesdropping on Lucy talking to the family who'd come to see Posy. They seemed nice – a couple, and their son, who looked about fourteen.

"Our lovely Jack Russell died three months ago," the lady was explaining. "He was twelve, so we should have expected it, I suppose. But it was still a shock. We weren't thinking of getting another dog, not for a while, anyway. But then we saw Posy in the paper…"

"She is lovely," Lucy agreed, smiling at Emily and Maya dithering by the hooks with the leads on, as though she could tell what they were trying to do. "Here's her pen, look."

Luckily Posy was on her best behaviour. She looked angelic, with her little brown ears pricked up excitedly, and her tail blurry with wagging. Even the boy, who'd been completely silent until now, crouched down and made a fuss of her, telling her how beautiful she was.

Emily and Maya exchanged relieved, triumphant looks, and headed off to walk the dogs.

"I just wish there were loads of nice families like that," Emily sighed, as they were dragged off towards the fields.

✦

"It's going to look amazing," Emily said admiringly, watching her mum smooth the green fondant icing over the huge cake. They'd made lots of cakes this week, and put them in the freezer ready for the party the next day, but this one was special.

Emily's mum had said that as it was the shelter's tenth birthday party, as well as a fundraiser, they really ought to have a special celebration cake. Emily had looked at her hopefully – her mum was brilliant at cakes. She made the best birthday cakes ever. Emily's last one had been a glittery ice rink with tiny icing people skating on it, because they'd taken her friends skating as a birthday treat.

"I don't suppose we could make one?" Emily had asked hopefully.

"Well, there is some of that special butter from the farm down the road left," her mum had pointed out. She was trying to sound as though she needed to be persuaded, but Emily knew she loved making cool cakes.

Quite a few people from school had bought tickets for the party – Mrs Angel the head had let the girls talk about it in assembly, and then sell tickets at lunch break the next day. So they had some money already to buy the things they needed – decorations, and the rosettes for the dog show, and most importantly, the ingredients for the party food. They'd made sure to put on all the posters that the food would be from local farms, and it was all organic, and animal-friendly, which meant that they had to search carefully for the best places to buy it. One of the farm shops had a bakery too, and were going to deliver twenty loaves of sliced bread to Maya's house the next morning – she had the biggest kitchen, and it was going to be turned into a sandwich production line.

"I think I'm going to try and keep on buying from that farm shop," Emily's mum said now, as she stood back and looked at the green cake. "I know it's more expensive, but the eggs were amazing. The cakes have turned out really well. And it's so good to think about the animals being really well looked after."

"Especially when you see those poor chickens at the shelter," Emily said, shuddering. "With all their feathers pecked out."

Her mum looked down at the cake. "Chickens! I wasn't going to put any chickens on it, do you think it matters? I've only made cats and dogs, and the guinea pigs."

"They're the best bit," Emily said, peeping into the ice cream tub where her mum had put the little icing models. "They're so cute. Although I love it that you made Barney and Whiskers and all the others. You really are clever, Mum."

PET PROTECTION

Her mum smiled. "It was fun – and you had all the photos, so it wasn't that difficult. It isn't as if I was trying to make models of them standing up, that would have been much harder. Once I've added a few little flowers, and some bunches of grass sticking up, hopefully it'll look like they're all just having a rest in the field."

"Mmmm, after they've all worn themselves out chasing each other," Emily said, giggling. "Oh, wow, I'd better go. I told Mrs Everett I'd be round to walk Charlie at three."

She hugged her mum, and let herself out of the back door, hurrying round the side of the house to the lane. She looked happily up at the wide stretch of blue sky. They'd been so lucky with the weather! She'd told the others that it always rained round her birthday and now they were in the middle of a heatwave. They needn't have worried about making sure they had somewhere to go if it was wet. Still – if it was as hot as this tomorrow, it would probably be good to have somewhere shady to sit.

She fetched Charlie from his house, and they set off to walk back up the lane towards the woods. Emily thought it would probably be cooler there. But by the time they were passing her house, Charlie was already panting, and she was wishing she'd brought a hat, and a bottle of water.

"Shall we stop and get them?" she said to Charlie, and he flapped his tail at her wearily. "You can have a nice big bowl of water too," she told him comfortingly. "I'll tie you up outside the back door. There's a good shady bit there."

Emily hurried into the house, and filled up an old plastic bowl with water, admiring the cake again as she went past. If she was quick, maybe she could help Mum put the cats and dogs on it later – Charlie wasn't going to want a really long walk in this heat.

By the sounds coming from upstairs, Mum was trying to get Sukie to have an afternoon nap, and it wasn't going very well. Toby and James were out in the garden somewhere – probably up the apple tree. She took the bowl of water outside, and Charlie started to gulp it down greedily. "I'll be back in a minute. I've just got to find my hat," she said, patting him.

Eventually Emily ran the hat down under her bed, covered in dust, and she dashed back down the stairs, hoping that Charlie hadn't got too impatient waiting, and started chewing on his lead or anything like that.

She could hear Toby and James from halfway

102

down the stairs. They were back in the kitchen now, and they were excited about something. Toby was doing that crazy laugh that made Mum really worry whenever she heard it. Emily sped up, but just as she came in the kitchen door, she saw Charlie dance into the kitchen, with his lead flapping loose.

"Why did you untie him?" she yelled crossly. "You should just have left him alone!" Then she gasped. Charlie had spotted the cake, and she was too far away to stop him. He jumped up at the table, his front paws actually *in* the cake, and turned his head sideways to wolf as much of it as he possibly could. "Get him down!" she wailed. But it was too late. The cake was ruined, and she could hear Mum coming down the stairs.

Quickly, Emily grabbed Charlie's collar, and hurried him outside, tying him to the fence. Then she went back into the kitchen, where her mum was staring at the cake, and James and Toby, obviously thinking that they had eaten it. For a minute, Emily was tempted to blame her brothers too. If she told Mum it was Charlie, it was just going to make her even more certain that they couldn't have a dog...

Emily sighed. Mum wasn't going to let them have one anyway, so it wasn't as if it mattered. "It wasn't them, Mum," she said sadly. "Well, it sort of was because they let Charlie off the lead. I'd tied him up in the garden while I came back to get my hat, and a drink for us both because it was so hot. He ate the cake."

"That lovely little spaniel?" Mum said, staring down at the gaping hole in the side of the cake.

"Mmmm. He likes cake." Emily sniffed. "I'm really sorry. I shouldn't have brought him into the garden." Her eyes filled with tears. "Do you think we could cut the eaten bit off?" she asked, gulping. "It was going to be so beautiful…"

"No…" Her mum shook her head. "No, I don't think we could, Ems. Not if we're going to serve it to people."

Emily nodded. She wanted to scream at Toby and James about how unfair it was and how they'd ruined everything, but somehow she was just too tired. She'd been dashing around organising things, and phoning people, and emailing newspapers all week. She just couldn't cope with anything else. What if this meant it was all going to go wrong? Emily slumped down on one of the kitchen chairs, and folded her arms on to the table.

"Hey… I only meant that we'd have to make

another one," her mum said gently. "We'll do the birthday cake, Ems, don't cry."

"Sorry, Ems," Toby said, looking at her worriedly. "We'll help."

"Go and finish walking Charlie," her mum told her. "Sukie isn't going to sleep, is she? We'll get her up and go and get the stuff we need from the farm shop instead. Then we can all make the new cake." She hauled Emily out of the chair. "Go on. Walk that dog. He needs to work off half a cake now, as well."

EIGHT

Emily raced back into the barn, looking for her mum. She'd been in there all afternoon, sorting out the teas, which had gone really well – everyone had loved the cakes, especially the new and improved unchewed birthday cake. Everyone had cheered, and they'd had to make an on-the-spot tombola to decide who got the slices with the different dogs and cats and guinea pigs.

But then there had been all the tidying up afterwards, while the girls organised the mask-making, and the games. Most of the volunteers from the shelter had been helping with the "Meet the Pets" sessions, with guinea pigs, and some of the calmer, friendlier dogs, so Emily's mum hadn't had a huge lot of help. Emily was sure she needed some time off.

"Mum! It's time for the dog show. It's going to be brilliant – you should see the costumes for the fancy dress. Do you want to go and watch it? If you tell me what to do, I can finish clearing up in here."

Her mum smiled at her. "You can't miss it, Ems. Anyway, I'm almost done. I was just making sure we'd put the paper plates in a recycling bag – Maya reminded me about that earlier on. I was just going to stuff it all into one to make it easier… But she came and helped – she even put all the leftover cucumber and carrot sticks in a bucket to take home. She said she was going to feed them to her worms? Does she have a worm tank, or something? I wouldn't have thought of her having pet worms, somehow…"

"It's a compost bin with worms in it," Emily told her mum, helping her sort through the bag of rubbish. "She showed me. It's quite cool, but it does smell. You know she's super-careful about recycling everything. She'd actually quite like to have a pig, so they can feed the rest of the food scraps to it, but then they'd have to make it into sausages when it got big, and Maya says she couldn't do it."

"I don't think I could, either," her mum agreed. "That's it – we're done! Let's go and watch the dog show."

Emily and the others had got up massively early that morning, because there were so many last-minute jobs to do – including making the ring for the dog show. Izzy's dad had lent them some sticks to bang into the ground, and some thin rope to wrap round them, so they could make a roped-off area for the dogs and owners to walk round. Lucy had quite a few big groundsheets and tarpaulins, so they'd put those down round the ring for the audience to sit on. The dog show was the last event of the day, and everyone seemed to be looking forward to it.

Emily's mum sat down with her dad and Sukie, Toby and James, and quite a lot of bits of cake. Emily hurried over to where Izzy was sitting at the corner of the ring, taking last-minute entries. She had a box in front of her full of pound coins – the dog show had been a fab fundraising idea, and quite a few people had brought their dogs and decided to enter on the day. Poppy had made a beautiful poster with pictures for all the different classes to go next to the ring – her waggiest-tail dog looked like it was about to take off. The rosettes for the winning dogs were pinned all along the bottom of the poster, too.

Maya was standing on a box at one side of the ring – they'd decided she had the loudest voice. Lucy and Mrs Everett were sitting on either side of her, wearing sashes, which Poppy had made, that said

108

PET PROTECTION

Judge. It all looked very official.

"Welcome to our dog show. The first class will be the musical sit. Please can all dogs entering come into the ring. And if you'd like to enter, and you haven't paid yet, please see Izzy over there!"

Poppy was sitting next to Mrs Everett with Maya's speakers and her iPhone. They'd downloaded a children's choir singing "How Much is that Doggy in the Window?" for the music, and then Maya's dad had suggested an Elvis song, "Hound Dog", as well.

"Everyone walks their dogs round the ring, and the last dog to sit when the music stops will be out," Maya explained, trying not to laugh as the very smart-looking Red Setter at the front of the line turned round to glare at the tiny dachshund who was trying to sniff his bottom. "Music!" she whispered to Poppy.

Lucy hurried over to the other side of the ring, so that she could see better, and the dogs set off. Emily watched anxiously as the music stopped, and Lucy and Mrs Everett looked to see who would be sent out of the ring. Their big worry with the dog show was that people (and dogs) might argue if they didn't agree with the judging. That was one reason Emily hadn't wanted to judge the different events themselves. She reckoned people were more likely to

109

argue with ten-year-olds. Mrs Everett could do a very headmistressy glare, and Lucy had a professional, don't-argue-I'm-a-judge face on, much stricter than she usually looked.

Luckily, the first dog's owner couldn't really disagree, since it was the dachshund, and he refused to sit down at all. "Never mind," his owner whispered to Emily as she hurried out of the ring. "You should see his costume for the fancy dress!"

In the end the smart Red Setter won – it was pretty impressive, actually, Emily thought, for a dog with such a lot of leg to sit down so quickly. She sighed. All the dogs' owners looked so proud of them, and there were lots who were younger than her. The Red Setter belonged to a boy in the year below her at school, who was delightedly fixing the red rosette on to the big dog's collar.

If only Charlie hadn't eaten the cake – this would have been such a good way to persuade Mum and Dad that they could have a dog. She smiled sadly as all the dogs lined up for the waggiest-tail competition, but then Izzy nudged her. "You're entering the next class, you'd better get ready!"

"What?" Emily stared at her.

"The sausage-catching! Mrs Everett organised it.

PET PROTECTION

She's got one of her friends who does dog-training classes to be a judge instead, so you and Charlie can enter without anyone saying it isn't fair. It's that lady over there, she's been looking after Charlie. Look! And hurry up, Maya's announcing the waggiest tail already!"

Emily turned to see Mrs Everett handing over her sash to another lady, who was beckoning her to take Charlie's lead.

"Good luck, Emily!" Mrs Everett said, laughing. "Not that I think you need it. Charlie's a natural. Although he'd be even better if it was cake, of course…"

Emily went pink. She'd told Mrs Everett what had happened – she'd had to, in case Charlie had made himself sick with too much cake. Luckily Lucy had opened the coolbox with the sausages, and Charlie yapped at her. He knew exactly what was happening, even if she didn't.

The dogs lined up, sitting next to their owners at the far end of the ring, and Lucy walked along, throwing sausages for them to catch – only the dogs who actually managed to jump and catch their sausages went through to the next round. A Jack Russell got disqualified for racing up to Lucy and just nicking sausages out of her hand, so there were only four in the first round. Emily was a bit worried that Charlie was smaller than the others – what if he couldn't jump to catch the sausage so well? Two of the dogs had already missed, and the dog next to them, who'd managed to catch his sausage, was a huge German shepherd. Emily was starting to see why dog owners argued about show entries – she felt like asking for Charlie to have a shorter throw. Or maybe a bigger sausage…

"Ready?" she whispered, as Charlie watched the German shepherd wolfing down his sausage, and he looked up at her, his ears pricked.

When Lucy threw the sausage at him, Charlie launched himself into the air, and caught it at the top of his leap. Emily was prepared to swear he'd actually eaten it by the time he hit the ground. Then he looked up at her smugly, as everyone clapped.

Lucy was much further away for the next round, and now there were only the two dogs left in. The German shepherd missed, and everyone gasped – but he didn't look very worried. He was quite happy to eat the sausage off the floor. Emily wondered worriedly if they had enough rosettes for a tie. Maybe she'd better just give the rosette to the German shepherd

112

if Charlie missed too.

Lucy threw the sausage a bit wide, and Emily was sure Charlie wouldn't get to it, but he managed an amazing sideways leap, and just reached it, snatching it out of the air as if he was the world's hungriest dog.

"You did it!" she told him, hugging him as he gobbled up the sausage and licked his whiskers smugly. It was definitely the best class to win, as far as Charlie was concerned. He hardly even noticed his rosette being tied to his collar, he was too busy making sure he hadn't missed any bits of sausage.

"Come on, you," Emily told him lovingly, as she took him over to sit at the side again. "We can watch the fancy dress now. I really want to see Billy – Poppy wouldn't say what he was going to be. Oh, and that dachshund…"

The fancy-dress dogs paraded into the ring, with all the audience laughing and cheering.

"Oh, wow!" Emily clapped loudly as Poppy walked past, with Billy dressed as a medieval horse, with an Action Man in cardboard armour on his back. His long nose was quite horsey, so he looked amazing, even though he was quite clearly sulking. Charlie jumped up excitedly and barked at the black Labrador who was following Billy, and Emily shuddered. The black dog was wearing a horribly realistic tarantula costume, with extra legs sticking out of a fluffy black waistcoat. The legs were bent at just the right angle, and it looked very spidery.

The dachshund was the best, though, and Emily was glad when Mrs Everett announced that he was the winner. He was a tan-coloured dachshund, so he did look quite like a sausage, and his costume was a bun. There was a bit of red and yellow fabric as the ketchup and mustard, and he looked like a huge hot dog on four little legs.

They'd decided that as quite a lot of people had entered the fancy dress, they'd better have second and third prizes as well, and Billy came second. The third prize went to a lurcher who was dressed as a three-headed dog, and he might well have beaten Billy and the sausage dog if he hadn't got sick of the whole fancy-dress thing and started eating one of his heads on the way round the ring.

Emily was clapping for Poppy and Billy when someone tapped her on the shoulder. "You were the winners for the sausage-catching, weren't you? Can I take your picture? I'm from the local paper."

"Oh! Yes, please." Emily scrambled up. "I'm really glad you came – I'm Emily Harris, it was me who

114

emailed you about the party. Thanks for putting so much in the paper about it – it made lots more people come."

The man smiled at her. "No problem. It made a fun article – all those great photos of the animals. Can you put your arms round him and smile? He's Charlie, isn't he?"

Emily did as she was told, and the man snapped several photos. "Great. That's all the winners, I think. Brilliant idea, the dog show. Especially the fancy dress. I took loads of those."

Emily looked at him thoughtfully. "Did you know that someone adopted one of those dogs that was in the article? Posy, the Jack Russell? They saw her in the paper, and went to the shelter. I don't suppose you could put more photos in the paper? Like – like a dog of the week? Or Kitten Corner, something like that? A Please Adopt Me page."

The man looked at her thoughtfully. "That's a good idea. I'll pass that on to the local reporter – she's the one who wrote the last article. I could get her to call you, could I?"

"Yes, or Lucy, she runs the shelter." Emily beamed at him. Lucy would be so excited.

"I'll do that. Thanks, then. Bye, Charlie." The

man stroked Charlie's beautiful curly ears. "You're lucky having him, he's cute. And a brilliant sausage-catcher!"

Emily almost started to explain that actually Charlie wasn't hers, she was just looking after him, but then she just smiled. She could pretend, just for once, couldn't she?

"Yes, he is," she said proudly. She scratched Charlie under the chin – his favourite place; scratching him there made him close his eyes and sigh blissfully. Then she shook herself. "Come on, sweetheart. We'd better give you back."

She looked around for Mrs Everett, and saw that she'd moved her folding chair over so she was sitting with Mum and Dad. Toby and James and Sukie were crowded round the sausage dog, admiring his costume, and petting him. Mum waved to her, and Emily forced herself to smile as she walked Charlie over.

"Well done!" Mrs Everett told her. "He looks lovely with his rosette on. I told you he'd win, didn't I?"

Emily nodded. "He's a natural, like you said."

"He could be a national champion," Emily's dad said, grinning. "You should take him to compete further afield!"

PET PROTECTION

Mrs Everett smiled. "Actually, that's the problem. It's getting difficult for me taking Charlie anywhere – that's why it's been so wonderful having Emily to walk him for me."

"I can take him out more days if you can't manage," Emily put in.

"It is getting harder." Mrs Everett sighed. "In fact, I need to ask you a huge favour."

"I love doing it, I don't mind," Emily told her. "I could come before school if you like."

"That wouldn't really help, Emily." Mrs Everett stroked Charlie, who was leaning against her, panting happily. "As I was just explaining to your parents, I'm afraid I'm going to have to move house. There are some flats closer into town – sheltered housing, you know. They're near to where my daughter lives, no stairs, someone around in case you fall. Very sensible, really. But no dogs allowed."

"Oh, no…" Emily whispered. "Will you have to take Charlie to the shelter?" She wasn't sure she could bear Charlie being there. Lucy and Emily and Maya and all the volunteers did their best, but Charlie was used to his own lovely home.

Mrs Everett looked between Emily and her mum and dad. "I'd hate that, but actually, I had a much better idea. I was hoping that I might be able to give him to you."

Emily gaped at her. It was the last thing she'd expected Mrs Everett to say. "But – but we can't have a dog... I'd love him, you know I would, but we don't have the room." *And he eats cakes*, she added sadly in her head.

"Well, we do really," her dad said, reaching out to rub Charlie's ears. "He's not huge."

Emily snapped her head round, staring at him in amazement. She'd expected her parents to say a grateful, polite, very firm no.

"But you always said... And Mum said... And he ate the birthday cake!"

Her mum was smiling. "We've been thinking about pets. You've worked so hard at the shelter, and with Charlie. You've looked after him beautifully. And he is usually very well-behaved, isn't he? The cake wasn't really his fault. I don't think he needs training at all, it should be James and Toby who have classes."

"You mean, we can really have him?" Emily whispered. She threw her arms around her mum and dad. "Oh, thank you! And thank you, Mrs Everett! You know I'll look after him for you, and bring him to visit..."

PET PROTECTION

Then she caught at Charlie's lead. He'd jumped up to sniff curiously at Billy's warhorse costume, as Poppy and Maya and Izzy came over.

"We've made fifty-six pounds just from the dog show!" Izzy told her.

"That's brilliant…" Emily stroked Charlie's rosette. She suddenly felt prouder of it than ever, now she knew that he was going to be hers.

"Altogether, we've definitely raised enough for the new roof. Lucy's so excited." Maya put an arm round her. "And my dad fell in love with the guinea pigs, so I can definitely have two as my birthday present. What are you looking all teary for? Are you OK? Is it because Charlie won?"

Emily nodded. "And because he's going to be my dog!"

Her friends looked at her in amazement. Then Izzy squealed and gave Emily a huge hug. Poppy and Maya joined in, and they all jumped up and down with excitement, while Charlie bounced around at their feet, barking delightedly.

Emily thought she might burst with happiness – the day had been a great success, the shelter would get a new roof, and best of all, she had a dog of her very own!

If you enjoyed this book,
then you'll love

the
PALOMINO
PONY
COMES
HOME

by

OLIVIA TUFFIN

Turn the page for a sneak peek!

PROLOGUE

"Just move, Lily. Go forward!" The rider's steely-blue eyes flashed angrily as she sat astride the golden palomino pony. She turned back to her mobile, but not before she had given the little mare a hefty kick.

The pony's nostrils flared and she snorted, but still she refused to walk on. Tentatively, she eyed the bushes ahead of her, her ears twitching back and forth.

"ENOUGH!" the girl cried. "Just do as I say!" With a loud thwack, she brought her riding crop down hard on the pony's hindquarters.

CRACK!

The mare wheeled round with a cry of pain that seemed to echo through the depths of the surrounding countryside. Then, just at that moment, a pheasant exploded out in front of them, squawking and flapping. Catching her footing on the hard, frozen tarmac the startled pony slipped, her hooves scrabbling and sparking.

"I said, go on!" the girl cried out. She struck the pony hard on her flanks again, frightening her even more. The mare reared in a moment of blind panic, tossing her head and showing the whites of her eyes.

The girl was thrown off clear into the road, rolling out of the way as the pony slipped on

to her side, scrambling and struggling on the muddy ground.

"Jemma … Jemma … are you all right?" A voice crackled through the mobile lying on the road.

As the girl lay winded and bruised, the pony scrabbled to her feet, her saddle slipping to one side and her reins broken.

Desperate to get away from the girl, the pony wheeled round and galloped wildly down the quiet road, veering on to a track that opened out to the moor beyond. With nothing to stop her, the pony raced and raced as if her life depended on it.

When she had covered at least three miles, the palomino finally slowed. She snorted into the clear crisp air, her breath hanging in a silver plume. She was safe at last.

CHAPTER ONE

"Phew, what a day that was!" Georgia slumped into her seat as the dark-green horse lorry pulled out of the showground. It was the first time she'd had a chance to relax all day, she'd been so busy grooming, plaiting and polishing. She hadn't actually ridden herself but she wasn't complaining. She loved being around horses and it was a real treat watching them compete.

Georgia especially loved Wilson, the big bay thoroughbred cross, and there was no doubt about it – he'd definitely been the star of the show! Georgia smiled as she pulled her tangled golden hair back into a ponytail. Wilson was owned by the Haydens – Sophie and her mother, Melanie – and was just one of the ponies that Georgia helped looked after in their yard.

"Thanks again for everything you've done today, Georgia," said Melanie as she drove the horse lorry down the bumpy old track and joined a long queue of horseboxes making their way home. "We couldn't have done it without you, could we, Sophs?" She turned to her daughter.

"Er, what was that?" Sophie looked up from the text she'd been busily composing.

"I said we couldn't have managed without Georgia's help today, could we?" Melanie frowned at her daughter, who was still engrossed in her phone.

"Er, no," Sophie mumbled. She was sitting between her mother and Georgia, a handful of rosettes spread across her lap.

Sophie sounded uninterested but Georgia knew that she wasn't being offhand. She just wasn't passionate about the looking-after part of being around horses, in the way that Georgia was. Sophie was going off to university next year, and at the moment her friends and her social life were probably more important to her than winning at the show.

Sophie finally pocketed her phone and grinned at Georgia. "I bet you'll be glad to see your bed tonight, eh, G?"

"You can say that again!" Georgia laughed. She was tired, but it was the best kind of tired. There was nothing she loved more than being at the

Haydens' yard and watching Sophie ride Wilson. Sophie was seventeen, three years older than Georgia, and she was already an amazing rider. Georgia hoped that one day she'd be as good.

"Well, I think you both did really well today," Melanie grinned. "A great team effort!"

Georgia smiled as she gazed out of the window, passing villages and fields. Today had been magical – the Wadebridge Show: a whole day to totally lose herself in horses. Georgia had wanted it to last for ever – not least because she knew that when she got home, she'd be thrown back into the reality of school and revision. Her end-of-year exams started tomorrow, and she hadn't done nearly enough work for them. "So how long will it take to get back?" she asked Melanie, biting down thoughtfully on her bottom lip.

"Probably a good couple of hours in this traffic," Melanie answered.

Georgia nodded. She'd thought as much. And once they were at the yard she'd have to help Sophie put Wilson to bed, unpack the lorry and do all the general tidying up before she could even think about any revision. Still, it was worth it. Helping out at the Haydens' was the closest that Georgia would get to ever owning her own pony and she relished every moment of it. Money had been tight in the Black household ever since her dad had left years ago and there was no way that her mum could afford the cost of expensive riding lessons, let alone the upkeep of a horse. If it hadn't been for all the riding that Melanie let her do in exchange for helping out at the yard, the only contact Georgia would get with ponies would be in her dreams!

Georgia turned to speak to Sophie, but the older girl's mobile had beeped and she was deep into her texting again.

Georgia smiled to herself. Oh, to live in Sophie's world where no matter what, the ponies would always be there…

CHAPTER TWO

Two hours later, and the horse lorry was turning up the drive to the Haydens' house. Redgrove Farm was a large modern building with stables attached, and fields and paddocks that stretched for as far as the eye could see. As the lorry drew to a halt in the yard, a tall, dark-haired man opened the front door.

"So, how did it go?" Simon Hayden asked.

"It was great, Dad," said Sophie, jumping down and pushing past him, nudging him affectionately as she went.

Sophie's dad rolled his eyes and gave Georgia a long-suffering grin as she got out of the horse lorry.

"Hey, hon," Melanie yawned, waving at her husband. Three noisy terriers yapped at her feet. "Get down, boys. Down!"

Georgia stretched – her arms and legs were stiff and aching. It was a lovely warm evening, the heat from the day still hanging in the air.

"Come on, Wilson, easy does it." Melanie soothed the bay gelding as she pulled down the ramp and led him into the yard. "Do you mind taking over, Georgia?" she asked, having glanced around for Sophie.

"Sure," said Georgia, taking the lead rope. "Come on, Wilson."

Once the thoroughbred cross was settled in his stable, Georgia ran over to a nearby barn to fetch a hay net. After giving him a final brush-down and checking he was fed and watered, she turned him out into the field for the night. She took off his head collar and put her arms around his neck, breathing in the gorgeous scent of horse mixed with citronella shampoo. "Off you go, boy," she murmured, patting his hindquarters.

Callie, Sophie's old pony, trotted eagerly over to join Wilson.

"Hello, you," smiled Georgia, giving the mousey dun pony a kiss on her nose.

Callie had been a champion pony in her time but she'd recently been retired. Georgia adored the little Exmoor pony that she'd learned to ride on.

Melanie and Georgia's mum were old friends, and after Lucy Black's husband left, she thought

taking her daughter over to Redgrove would be a good distraction. Georgia had immediately loved the ponies and as soon as her mum thought she was old enough, Melanie had started to lead her round the paddock on Callie. And the rest was history! Redgrove had quickly become a home-from-home for Georgia.

"You look very thoughtful." Melanie came up behind Georgia, breaking the spell.

"Oh," Georgia said with a smile. "I was just remembering the first time you put me on Callie."

Melanie patted her on the arm affectionately. "That seems like yesterday!" She smiled warmly. "I can drop you home if you like."

"Really? That would be great, thanks," said Georgia. "You've remembered that I can't come up here after school this coming week, haven't you? Exams."

"Yes, I know," said Melanie. "What will we do without you?"

"You'll manage just fine." Georgia grinned, feeling secretly pleased by Melanie's words.

"When the exams are over you'll have Wilson all to yourself, you know," Melanie continued.

"Really?" Georgia was surprised.

"Yes," said Melanie. "Just for a few days during the first week of the holidays. Sophie's got a job at a local summer camp. So you can exercise him every day if you want to."

"*If* I want to!" cried Georgia, rushing over to give Melanie a massive hug. "I can't wait!"

Melanie smiled. "Simon," she called over her shoulder to her husband. "I'm just going to drop Georgia back." She pulled out the car keys from her pocket and walked over to a shiny new four-by-four that was parked in the yard.

Georgia sighed. Oh, to live like the Haydens.

Not only did they have the most amazing stables for their horses, but their grounds had a swimming pool and a tennis court too. Still, they worked hard for their lifestyle and were very down-to-earth and friendly.

As the four-by-four splattered down the lane, Georgia thought about home. What would her mum be up to at that moment? Probably still painting, as she was busy with an important commission. Georgia's mum was an artist and worked every possible hour to make ends meet. When Georgia had left early that morning for the show, she was up and already absorbed in her latest picture.

The four-by-four turned the corner at the end of the bumpy lane and on to the main road, its headlights lighting up the twilight. After about a mile, they pulled up outside a cottage.

"Thanks, Melanie," said Georgia as she jumped

out of the car. She gave her mum's friend a wave before turning to walk up the path.

The house was quiet when Georgia opened the front door. As she entered the kitchen she could just about hear the faint sound of the radio coming from the shed at the end of the garden where her mother worked.

Dumping her stuff on the kitchen table, Georgia ran over the small lawn. Pip, her faithful black and white spaniel who had been dozing in the last of the evening sunshine, sprang up to greet her, her tail thumping.

"Hi, Mum," she called, poking her head round the door of the shed.

"Oh, hello, sweetheart." Georgia's mother looked up. "I must have lost track of the time." She pushed back a stray piece of hair that had fallen across her face and smoothed her paint-splattered apron. "Have you had a good day?"

"Yes, great, thanks." Georgia bent down to give her mum a kiss. "Have you eaten?"

"Just a sandwich," her mother answered. "I grabbed one earlier. What about you?"

"I had something at the show," said Georgia.

"So? How did they do?" her mum asked.

"Two firsts and three seconds." Georgia grinned.

"Fantastic!" her mum enthused. "But you look shattered, love. It's bed for you now. You need an early night for school tomorrow."

School. Georgia groaned but she knew her mum was right. "OK, Mum," she said.

"Did you get some revision done in the horse lorry like you promised?" her mum asked.

"Yes," Georgia said, crossing her fingers behind her back.

"That's good." Lucy Black nodded as Georgia hurried back to the cottage and up the stairs.

Once Georgia was in her tiny room, where

every surface was decorated with photos and posters of horses or her mum's paintings, exhaustion swept over her. It was no good – she couldn't revise now. She'd have to get up early and do a bit of work in the morning. Trying not to look at the pile of school books stacked precariously on her desk, Georgia put on her pyjamas and sank gratefully into bed.

She fell asleep instantly and was soon dreaming about her favourite thing in the world – ponies! Beautiful bay hunters with smooth paces, little hacks with flowing manes, and flashy showjumpers flying over fences...